Lila Fowler, movie star?

"So you're really making a movie?" Lila asked Sam.

"Yeah, uh . . ." Sam hesitated. What was Princess Lila doing in this low-rent film shop?

"*I* want to be the star of it, Sam," Lila said. "What do you say?"

Sam was about to say that his movie was a *documentary,* and even so, he wouldn't cast Lila Fowler in a million years. But as he looked her over, in her sexy jeans and her tight ribbed turtleneck, plus the black sunglasses covering half of her face, he had to admit that she looked like a movie star on a weekend.

"Lila, why do you even want to be in my little movie?" Sam asked.

"Oh, I have my reasons, Sam." Lila waved a platinum credit card under his nose. "So what's it going to be? Do I pay for the camera lens you really want and I become the star of the movie? Or do I walk away with my Visa and you buy that pathetic lens and cast someone a lot less attractive in your film?"

Without another word Sam snatched the card out of her fingers and handed it to the man behind the counter.

Lila smiled.

Bantam Books in the Sweet Valley University series.
Ask your bookseller for the books you have missed.

And don't miss these Sweet Valley University Thriller Editions:

Visit the Official Sweet Valley Web Site on the Internet at:
www.sweetvalley.com

SWEET VALLEY UNIVERSITY®

SECRET
LOVE
DIARIES

Sam

Written by
Laurie John

Created by
FRANCINE PASCAL

BANTAM BOOKS
NEW YORK · TORONTO · LONDON · SYDNEY · AUCKLAND

SECRET LOVE DIARIES: SAM

A Bantam Book / November 2000

*Sweet Valley High® and Sweet Valley University®
are registered trademarks of Francine Pascal.
Conceived by Francine Pascal.*

*Copyright © 2000 by Francine Pascal.
Cover art copyright © 2000 by 17th Street Productions,
an Alloy Online, Inc. company.*

Produced by 17th Street Productions,
an Alloy Online, Inc. company.
33 West 17th Street
New York, NY 10011.

ISBN: 0-553-49351-5

Visit us on the Web! www.randomhouse.com/teens

Published simultaneously in the United States and Canada

Bantam Books is an imprint of Random House Children's Books, a
division of Random House, Inc. BANTAM BOOKS and the rooster
colophon are registered trademarks of Random House, Inc. Bantam Books,
1540 Broadway, New York, New York 10036.

PRINTED IN THE UNITED STATES OF AMERICA

OPM   0 9 8 7 6 5 4 3 2 1

To Gabriel Markowitz

SECRET
LOVE
DIARIES

Sam

Chapter One

FROM SAM BURGESS'S THOUGHT BOOK . . .

What is it with girls? They think guys are shallow? Ha. You are not going to believe what just happened to me. I'm not sure I believe it myself. I'm still getting over it. I don't know whether to laugh, cry, or shove my skull through the wall. Dig this:

I was out in front of the house just now, minding my own business, not hurting anyone, washing my car. Sudsy wudsy, splish splash, soapy, rinsy, wax on, wax off, the whole deal. One hour to gleaming wheels. A local band was practicing in the garage a few houses down; you'd think they were the Backstreet Boys the way one cute girl after another came down our little street to watch them play.

So one girl, an adorable brunette, seemed to be checking me out and smiling shyly, so I said hi, and we started talking. And then she asked me if I belonged

1

to a frat at Sweet Valley University (which tipped me off that this cutie might not be my kind of girl). So I said no, I go to Orange County College, otherwise known as OCC.

Wrong!!! *As in* wrong *answer.* I might as well have told her I had some horrible contagious disease or something. Her smile went away, she crossed her arms, and I swear a cloud went in front of the sun. And you know what she said? Did she say, "Oh, that's cool?" Did she say, "Oh, what's that like?" No. She said (and I am not making this up), "Oh. I see."

I see? What exactly did she see? That my little beat-up car wasn't that cute anymore? That I must be low-rent because I went to a community college and not big-deal Sweet Valley University? That I suddenly had a big L on my forehead? What a snob. Anyway, here's what she said next: "Um, well, nice talking to you. But I gotta go. My boyfriend's waiting for me."

My boyfriend. Yeah, right. And I wanted to say, you *stopped* to talk to me, remember? And I know you don't have a boyfriend, or at least not one you like enough to not *flirt* with me. Maybe I don't know all the answers about the female mind, but I'm smarter than any guy who goes to SVU, which means I knew when a girl was lying to me. So I just went back to waxing off the hood 'cause it wasn't like there was anywhere for me to go to get out of that awkward sitch 'cause, duh, I'm home already.

2

*At least I found out soon enough that she's a snob.
I hate to think what would have happened if we'd
been out somewhere and she'd found out that I don't
attend the great genius factory that is Sweet Valley
Loserversity. No, I just go to Orange County College,
home of the Fightin' Morons, where they teach young
dipsticks to dress themselves, count to ten without taking their shoes off, and ask, "So, you want fries with
that?" I'd hate to see that look on her face over beer
and darts. 'Cause bro, that would have been uncomfortable. That would have been ugly.*

*But whatever. I know the scenario. This isn't the
first time I've been dissed for my choice of educational
institutionalization. It's all good. If some folks have
the deep pockets of Mommy and Daddy to pour into
SVU's bank account, that's all right with me; I'm not
prejudiced. I know they look down on us, some of them,
but not all, and that's my choice, and that's their
choice, you know? For some reason, maybe because I
wasn't expecting anything, and maybe because she
came up to me instead of me to her, and maybe because I really just wanted to wash my car, I didn't
give it another thought. I just felt sorry for her. Toodle-
oo, sweet cheeks.*

*And then, not five minutes later, here comes the
second lovely. Finer. Not a granola type like the first
but a sizzling city mamacita, with short shorts and a
string-back halter, just the kind I like. And just like*

3

before, I don't know, maybe I ought to soap up the ride more often 'cause she's up on me even before I know she's there. I'm down on the ground, picking grit out of my wheels with a wire brush, and this honey just up and outs with, I swear, "Now, why don't all guys have that attention to detail?" And duh, you cannot go wrong with a line like that. So we're talking about this and that, and thought book o' mine, I must be sending off some kind of crazy scent or something because everything I say is going over like Austin Powers, 'cause she's laughing at all the right places like we're old buddies, and it turns out her name is Jenny, and she likes my name too (right—she likes "Sam"), and then she wants to know what year I am at SVU. So I tell her I'm a sophomore, but, and whoops, here it comes: that I don't go to SVU. And then she looks confused, like, well, then, what are you doing here? Like I should have been wearing a label: *Warning: Do not approach unless you can handle that this guy doesn't go to SVU.*

So I try to explain it to her in words she can get her head around. I tell her I go to OCC and ask if she's heard of it, if she knows where the school is. And yeah, she says, she knows where it is. She knows where the town dump is too, her eyes say. At least she didn't say she had a boyfriend. All she said was, "Well, it was nice meeting you," and she was gone. Nice meeting me. Yeah. You too.

Thought book, ol' buddy, is there something I don't know about OCC? It's not a halfway house for psychos, at least not that they've told me. It seems all right to me. Heck, I like OCC. OCC is great. OCC has been very good to Sam Burgess. OCC is a friend in need. It was there for me when I needed a supercheap school 'cause I am not going to take my parents' money for anything, even college. And I needed a college that would let me in when my high-school grades weren't that good, and my teachers didn't exactly think I was going to be the next Bill Gates, and they were ready to say so to anybody who asked. So I cut a lot of classes in high school; what's the big deal?

I had a lot of thinking to do on my own, and if my thinking had been about trigonometry, well, I would have gone to trig class to do it, but it wasn't about the arc secant of the cosine of the hypotenuse; it was mostly about people, real people, the people I didn't understand but wanted to. And I didn't hear a lot about real people in high school, so I had to do my thinking on my own, okay? You gotta do what you gotta do. So I wasn't Mr. Valedictorian, I was Mr. Might Not Graduate, but hey, even us class cutters need a place to get higher educated, so it was OCC for me, and it's cool with me, and I'm cool with it. But I'm still a person—*not that you could convince Hottie #1 or Hottie #2 of that. To them, OCC is where the roaches come from.*

I guess it isn't about learning around here; it's about getting on the good side of the social divide. It isn't about being real, about being a genuine person, about figuring things out on your own. It's about relying on Mommy and Daddy to set you up, like the Wakefield twins do, about sorority rushes and Frisbee on the quad with Biff and Bunny and grade grubbing to get into medical school and making connections with the other preppies so you'll know them when it comes time to get accepted to the yacht club. In other words, it's not about me. And that's cool with me in the end, all right—you be you, and I'll be me, and that's the way it was meant to be, isn't it? So why does everyone make me feel like I'm trying to get away with something? Like they're saving the planet and I'm burning Styrofoam and dumping toxic waste in the lake?

Okay, it's not like it's everyone. Some SVU people are pretty cool. I have to admit, for all the noise I put up with from the Goldilocks duo, they've never made me feel like I'm a bad person just because I don't go to SVU. For all her tiresome whining Elizabeth Wakefield has turned out to be a pretty good person. I have to admit that she's sincere, and even when she criticizes me, I can tell she cares. And Neil Martin's all right. He's in the same boat as me financially, getting disowned by his narrow-minded parents for being gay, like that was something he had any choice about or

6

like he was doing it just to make them mad. They're worse than my parents when you get down to it. Neil's cool, and I'm glad I got to have him as a housemate 'cause he's taught me a lot and he's fun to hang out with, and besides, he gets in as many shots at Elizabeth and her twin, Jessica, as I do. It's nice to have another guy around who isn't all gaga at the sight of a blond mane.

Well, I guess I was pretty steamed after getting blown off the second time because I decided to put another coat of wax on the old bucket of bolts. I was thinking about whether I should get T-shirts made up that say, No, I Do Not Attend Sweet Valley University, and just then, like someone was playing some kind of cosmic joke on me, a throaty, sexy voice came from behind me, saying, "Cute car."

This time I was prepared. I wasn't even surprised to look up and see this completely gorgeous girl, this supercutie, standing there in a red sundress, her hands on her hips and a smile on her ruby lips. She made the first two look like obnoxious little girls who just lost the spelling bee and were going home to play with Barbie dolls. She looked like she could chew me up and spit me out and I would love every minute. It was like she came from a dream. A nice dream.

But dude, fuggedaboudit, there's only so much a man can take. I wasn't falling for it again. I let her have it. "Sorry," I said, "I don't think I'm your type."

7

And I said "type" like I was spitting a bug out of my mouth. I mean, I was going to get out of it first this time because I am not interested in being a three-time loser in one afternoon.

Well, she looked like this was the first time anyone had ever blown her off like that, right off the bat, 'cause she just stood there with her hands stuck on her hips and her face frozen with her mouth open and her eyes wide and round. And dude, I did not look twice, I just went right back to my buff rag because I was going to get out of there before the next homecoming queen came down the pike. I never thought I would be running away from pretty girls, but live and learn, my thought book, live and learn.

She didn't say another word, thank goodness, didn't even ask me if I went to SVU or if I went to reform school. I don't know what she thought, and I don't care. I didn't even hear her walk away on those killer legs of hers. I just went back to work with the buff rag, and all I got for my afternoon of work is a supershiny car that still sounds like it swallowed a bag of sand and a bad mood. I have got to stop talking to SVU chicks. If Sam ain't good enough for them, that's fine. Who needs 'em? There are babes in every one of my OCC classes to choose from, and at least they won't look down on me for sitting next to them in our humble college.

But that'll have to come up next time. I'm in my

*American-lit class right now, and the prof is star-
ing at me and wondering when I started taking
such copious notes.*

Nineteen-year-old Sam Burgess sat on the couch
in the living room of his way-off-campus (for OCC,
not SVU) living room, his thumbs working furi-
ously over the Sony Playstation control pad, his eyes
glued to the TV screen.

"Blam! Blam blam blam!" The fiery missiles spat
from Lara Croft's weapon to destroy the targets
that appeared one after the other in her sights.

Sam jerked upward as the helpless enemies ex-
ploded as soon as they appeared. "Ha!" he cried.
"Eat hot lead!" But suddenly someone threw a
denim jacket over Sam's head. "Hey!" he yelled, his
sandy brown head shaking free. "What's the deal!"
He threw off the jacket and turned around to find
his housemate Neil Martin grinning at him.

"Sam!" Neil exclaimed in mock surprise. "I
didn't see you there!"

Sam stared at his housemate in disbelief, the
game controller hanging from his hand by the wire,
dangling like a mobile. "Whaddaya mean, you
didn't see me?" he wailed in disbelief. "How could
you not see me?"

"Sorry, Sam," Neil posited, running a hand
through his dark hair, the sarcasm in his gray eyes

now revealing false concern. "It's just that, well, you're starting to blend into the furniture. I guess you just looked like a part of that couch to me. When something is always planted in the same place, it doesn't look like a person anymore; it just looks like . . . well . . . a table or something. A lamp."

Sam was not amused. He contemplated the screen glumly, the high score no consolation. Just when he was making progress into completely new territory!

"You know, Mulder," Neil intoned huskily, presenting a passable imitation of Gillian Anderson, Dana Scully on the *X-Files*, "despite the rumors and legends surrounding the supposed figure of Sam Burgess, there's little evidence that such a creature actually exists!" Neil adopted a bored expression. "C'mon, Scully," he said, switching to the nasal muttering of David Duchovny, aka Fox Mulder, "people have been talking about the Phantom Slacker around these parts for generations! Beer and food disappear mysteriously, and how do you explain that smell of unwashed laundry that's always emerging from the 'Sam room' in the back of the house?"

Sam made a yeah-like-you're-funny face at Neil. But Neil, apparently, was enjoying his little skit.

"I'm sure there's a scientific explanation, Mulder," Neil continued as Scully, unmoved by the scowl he met on Sam's face. "Look at the facts: Has this 'Sam' ever been seen actually sleeping in what his roommates call his bed? No, he hasn't. The stories of nighttime liaisons with strange women or crashing at his thick-skulled, so-called buddies' places are just that: stories. There's no hard proof the Slacker ever spends a night in the room devoted to him. And look at the legend more closely: He's supposed to be a student, but none of his professors report seeing any evidence of schoolwork. Doesn't sound like a student to *me*. Wouldn't you think that after all this time, we'd be able to find one paper, one test, even a book checked out of the library?"

Neil was on a roll. He switched back to Mulder, protesting against Scully's rigid empirical mind. "C'mon, Scully, maybe he does his research on the Internet!"

"I thought of that, Mulder," Neil went on, getting very close to the character of the hardheaded scientist. "I looked at the Web browser on his computer, and its history files reveal nothing but dirty-joke pages and dormitory Web cam sites! And look—if he actually lived here, if he was a real person, you'd think he'd do some household chores from time to time. Wash the dishes, vacuum, clean the bathroom, *something*. But no, everything goes untouched. I'm sorry, Mulder, but without some real evidence I'm going to have to conclude that the Phantom Slacker is just that—a phantom!"

Sam lay down on his back on the couch, turning his face away from Neil, and pretended not to hear him. Neil wasn't to be stopped, though. "But Scully, how about the smells and the noises? No phantom could generate those horrible phenomena!"

"No, Mulder, but animals could. Why, a colony of rats, a dog, maybe a few goats? It's not out of the question."

Sam sighed in defeat. "All right, all right," he said. "Maybe I need to get out a little more, and I was just about to do the breakfast dishes. Don't be so hard on me. It's only two o'clock."

"Yeah, Sam." Neil smiled, gloating in the triumph of his sarcasm. "But the dishes are from breakfast *Tuesday*. I barely persuaded Jessica this morning not to put them in your bed."

"Well, I do too do schoolwork." Sam reached for a last resort.

"Hardly." Neil clucked. "You don't seem to be taking much of an interest in anything around you these days. You're bored. And you know what happens to people when they're bored? They get boring."

Sam couldn't think of anything to say. He was hardly going to defend his professors or classes to Neil, especially considering all the complaining he'd been doing to himself about their lameness. "Well," he said, "at least you're wrong about me sleeping here. I haven't managed to spend the

12

night in another person's room in a long time."

"Yeah, Sam, I guess you're right," Neil allowed. "You do sleep."

That hadn't had quite the effect Sam had hoped for. He gave up arguing with Neil. Tomb Raider had lost its appeal for the moment. He wanted to get out of there. "Here's your·coat." He dropped Neil's jacket behind the couch.

He wasn't in the mood to be slammed by his own housemate and buddy, no matter how right Neil might be.

Was he right?

Sam was so used to being told what to do, how to do it, and that his way was the wrong way by his family that he figured everyone who had something to tell him was as wrong as they were. Anyway, why couldn't Sam just be himself? Why did everyone have to get on his case? If it wasn't the school he chose to go to, it was his sloppy habits or passion for video games.

He was a good guy. Sam knew he was, and that was all that mattered.

He was a good guy. Right?

Sam slouched from the bathroom toward the kitchen. He was dreading the enormous pile of dishes waiting for him in the sink. Had they really been there since Tuesday? *Wait a second, what day is it now?* he wondered. He thought it was Friday, but

13

he couldn't be completely sure. No, it was Thursday. One more day until the weekend.

So maybe Neil was right about one thing after all. Maybe he did need to get out more. And maybe he needed to start paying a little more attention to school too. But all his classes were just so . . . so boring. Just like Neil had said. Sam was bored, and now he was afraid that he was becoming *boring* too.

Well, it wasn't like his housemates were exactly the most exciting people in Sweet Valley either. What were they doing that was so much more important and interesting than keeping one's car clean and honing one's video-game skills? Nothing, he decided. Nothing at all.

"Wow, that sounds so cool!" Neil gushed at Elizabeth Wakefield just as Sam walked into the room. "I didn't know that you got to do a stint at student teaching as part of advanced sociology. Is that, like, a requirement for the course?"

Elizabeth used a perfectly manicured hand to brush a long, golden lock of hair away from her blue-green eyes. She sat across the kitchen table from Neil and didn't bother acknowledging Sam as he made his entrance. "Not everyone has to do student teaching," Elizabeth explained. "There were a bunch of different choices for our final project, and I don't know, the teaching thing just sounded really interesting and fun. So I'll assist the teacher for

14

six weeks, and then I write a report on it."

"That is so great." Neil reached across the table to touch Elizabeth's arm. "But isn't it scary?"

"What, teaching?" Elizabeth sounded surprised.

"No, not teaching, silly," Neil answered. "Although I'm not sure I could get up in front of a bunch of third graders every day. But I was talking about South-Central. I've never even driven into that part of Los Angeles—it has a really scary reputation. You're not nervous about going over there?"

"I don't know; I haven't been to the school yet," Elizabeth answered thoughtfully. "I guess I never really considered it. But I doubt my professor would send me someplace that wasn't safe."

Sam ignored the dishes for the time being and listened in on Elizabeth and Neil's conversation. Neither of them had spoken to him since he entered the room. Sometimes it did feel like he was invisible inside this house. Sam wondered if they were still holding grudges about him not helping out more with the chores.

"Yeah, I'm sure it'll be fine," Neil said in response to Elizabeth.

"So, tell me about your first day at the station, Neil." Elizabeth shifted the subject as she leaned slightly toward Neil. "Do they have you reading the news yet?"

"No, they started me out on traffic," Neil

answered. "So they took me up in the helicopter this morning, and I delivered the entire LA freeway report."

"Shut up!" Elizabeth shouted. "You did not."

Neil answered with a sly smile. "So I guess you're not as gullible as you used to be, eh, Elizabeth?"

"Yeah, well, I think living with you and Sam has helped a lot in that respect," Elizabeth answered, finally glancing up to acknowledge Sam standing in the middle of the kitchen. "Hey, Sam. How's virtual reality?"

"I'm not even going to ask you what that's supposed to mean," Sam responded defensively. He was beginning to feel like he was the butt of an in-house joke about his lack of life. He resisted making a crack about Neil riding shotgun in News 2 Chopper 1.

Elizabeth turned back to Neil. "So, really, how'd it go today?"

"It was cool." Neil shrugged. "They basically just gave me a tour around the newsroom, showed me the equipment, and introduced me to people."

"Oh, dude," Sam interjected. "Did you get to meet that new weather girl, Heather Chatterjee? She is so hot!"

"Yeah, she is a cutie, huh, Sam?" Neil answered with a raised eyebrow. "I didn't meet her, but when I do, I'll see if I can get her to autograph an eight-by-ten glossy for you, okay, bud?"

"Oh, that would be dreamy, Neil," Sam answered in a fake swoon.

"But I did meet Chuck Cameron, sports," Neil offered.

"Oh, that dude's a chump," Sam scoffed.

"I think he's cute," Elizabeth argued.

"Me too," Neil agreed. "And I heard he's gay too."

"He is not gay," Sam insisted. "I heard he was dating that chick from *Live at Five*."

"That doesn't mean he isn't gay," Neil pointed out. "But I'm not really into sports that much anyway."

"Well, let me know if you can hook me up with Lakers tickets," Sam answered hopefully.

"Yeah, right." Neil smirked. Then he addressed Sam as he would a small child. "But if you're really nice and clean your room, I'll see if I can get you into a Clippers game."

"The Clippers?" Sam asked in disgust. "You'd have to pay me to go to a Clippers game!"

"Hey, there's a job for you, Sam," Elizabeth offered sarcastically. "Maybe you *could* get paid to watch basketball games. It would be even better if you could do it at home. Then you'd never have to leave your beloved couch."

Sam chose to ignore Elizabeth's dig and was relieved to hear the door open. Maybe Jessica's arrival would provide a respite from hearing about all of Neil's and Elizabeth's important extracurricular activities. His relief faded when he heard two voices chirping through the front room: Jessica's and her snobby friend Lila Fowler's.

The two of them bounced into the room, looking purposeful with their book bags and bottled water.

"Hey, Lizzie, hi, Neil," Jessica greeted cheerfully. Her voice turned closer to a sigh or a groan when she looked at Sam. "Hi, Sam."

"It's so nice to see you too, Jessica," Sam answered in the fakest friendly voice he could muster.

"Lila, you're looking lovely as usual," he added, sounding only slightly less phony as he looked Lila over, from her model-straight-to-the-shoulders chestnut hair down to her black sandals. Along the way he lingered on her tight, black baby T-shirt and black drawstring pants. In small, pale pink letters across her well-endowed chest read: *Princess*.

"I see that someone has finally designed a T-shirt especially for you," Sam noted dryly.

Lila shot Sam an accusatory glance. "And?"

"And, um . . ." Sam paused, suddenly at a loss for words in the face of Lila's stunning good looks and icy attitude. "All righty, then."

"All righty, then," Lila mocked.

"Don't worry about him." Neil spoke from his seat at the table. "Sam sometimes has trouble communicating after spending so many hours playing video games."

"Oh, I'll be fine, Neil, thanks," Lila answered evenly.

Jessica nodded toward Sam and spoke in an amplified whisper to Lila. "We find it's best if you just ignore him."

"So, what are you guys up to?" Elizabeth asked her twin sister.

"Omigod, we have so much work to do," Jessica answered, her eyes bulging. "We have to, like, completely plan the Theta rush week. There's all these events we have to organize, and we've got to get the invitations together and then figure out which girls are even going to get invitations."

"Wow, that does sound like a lot of work," Neil remarked.

"Oh, it totally is, but it's fun, really," Jessica answered happily. "It's just a big party, you know?"

Jeez, Sam thought, *even Jessica is doing something with her time besides flirting with guys.*

Jessica looked at Sam. "So what are *you* up to, Sam?" It sounded more like a challenge than a simple question. And Sam wasn't about to take her up on it. He had already had enough abuse from his housemates for one afternoon.

"Nothing," he answered flatly. "Absolutely nothing."

"Oh, come on, Sam," Jessica teased. "You must have something going on in your life. I mean, you go to school, don't you? Or did you drop out already?"

Before Sam could think of something self-deprecating to say, Lila did it for him. "Sam goes to OCC, don't you remember, Jessica? There's no point in dropping out of OCC because it's not even a real school to begin with. I mean, I don't even think it's *accredited*—whatever that means."

Lila's lame explanation set off a few minor chuckles in the peanut gallery, but Sam wasn't laughing. He just glared at Lila. Without fully realizing what was happening, the glare shifted to full-blown ogling. She was definitely hot, that much was certain. But so completely not his type. Her T-shirt said it all. She was a total princess. She was one of the, if not *the*, richest girls in Sweet Valley. Still, he began to wonder what it would actually be like to snag a chick like the queen of the rich snobs, Lila. *That would show my I'm-so-great housemates*, Sam thought. His eyes returned to linger on her T-shirt, and he wasn't exactly reading the words anymore.

Lila caught him checking her out and rolled her eyes as if to say, "Dream on, slacker."

It didn't take much for Sam to read her mind. He answered her telling look with a simple three-word response: "You wish, Fowler."

"Yeah, right." Lila smirked back at him. She shook her head, as if to take pity on a lesser being who was confused by human customs.

Sam took the exchange as a cue to return to his one true love, the only girl who truly understood him: Lara Croft, queen of the video game. She never gave him grief.

Okay, Thought Book, it looks like it's just you and me now. You, me, and Lara. Slacker Sam, his virtual girlfriend, and dear, dear Diary. For a guy who does absolutely nothing with his time, I've sure got a lot to say, huh? So now I'm talking to a notebook? Oh, yeah, that's the idea.

So I guess my housemates aren't so cool about me going to OCC after all. I guess they're just like all those stuck-up hotties who dissed me while I was washing my car. OCC isn't a real school. Huh! Oh, wait. That was Lila who said all that crap about OCC. No wonder: She's a hottie but a total snob with her nose in the air just like those girls I met on the street.

Now that I think about it, the three upstanding citizens who live in this house with me didn't have a thing to say about my substandard institution of education. They chuckled a little, sure. But those three usually just bust my chops for my lack of motivation, the hours I spend in front of the tube, and my nonexistent housekeeping skills.

And maybe they're right. And maybe they are leading more productive lives than I am. Elizabeth, with her dedication to school and her new student-teaching assignment that now allows her to make an even greater contribution to society. And now Neil has his internship at the TV station (he's thinking about becoming a political commentator), bringing the world closer to us all. And then there's Jessica. Not that being in a sorority is anything worthwhile. But at least she does stuff. And she's probably making those all-important social contacts that will set her up for life.

So maybe I should listen to Neil. Maybe I should get off my lazy butt and start winning at something other than Sony Playstation. But what? I'm not into anything enough to waste my time pursuing it seriously. I mean, it's not like I'm going to make it on the professional-darts circuit. And I guess playing video games isn't exactly a path to enlightenment either. So what am I supposed to do?

And what's everyone else trying so hard to prove anyway? That they exist? Well, I'm not falling into that trap. I do exist. And here's the proof, right in front of me: words on paper.

So what's the point in writing down my thoughts if they're never going to lead me into action?

Why can't people just leave me alone? I can tell that Elizabeth is busy judging me all the time. And even though she doesn't come right out and say it, I can tell she's somehow disappointed in me. I hate that. What does she care what I do with my life?

And who does Lila think she is anyway? Princess is

right. She thinks she can go around putting people down and getting everything she wants just because her rich daddy pays her way through life? Well, maybe I have a rich daddy too. But that wouldn't give me the right to think I'm God's gift to the world. And I wouldn't want his stinky old money anyway. I can make it on my own in this world. Whether I make something of myself or not.

Whoa. All this talk of ambition—or lack thereof— is making me thirsty. Hey, there's something I'm good at: drinking beer.

Chapter Two

Sam closed his journal and slid it under a pile of magazines on his bedside table. He slipped his feet into his well-worn pair of flip-flops and flippity-flopped into the kitchen. He was grateful to see that the recent meeting of the we-all-think-Sam-is-a-pathetic-loser club had adjourned, and he had the entire kitchen, complete with sink full of festering dishes, all to himself.

Sam pulled open the refrigerator door with a sense of doomed resignation. He knew the answer before his eyes could ask the question. No beer. So that settled it. He wouldn't be able to do the dishes after all. His thirst came first. And he wasn't thirsty for mere water or orange juice. He had to have beer. And he needed to get out of the house anyway, right? Wasn't that what Neil had told him?

Of course Sam knew the perfect place to go: his favorite neighborhood bar, The Burgundy Room. The primary reason that The Burgundy Room was his favorite watering hole was location. And it wasn't the fact that it was on the SVU campus—that type of proximity he could live without. What really mattered was that it was the closest bar to his house.

Sam ducked back into his room to grab some cash and considered whether or not he should put on some actual shoes. *Nah, who needs shoes?* He was only walking two blocks, and besides, The Burgundy Room felt like an extension of his living room. Sam glanced in the mirror above his dresser, mainly to make sure he didn't have pen marks on his face. It wasn't like he put much thought into the rest of his appearance, he suddenly realized. He glanced at his baggy green shorts and his faded T-shirt. He wasn't going to put on proper shoes, so what was the point of changing his clothes? If everyone was going to think he was a slacker, he might as well dress the part, right?

A minute later he was out the door and had covered the few blocks to the bar. For a fleeting moment Sam had second thoughts about his attire when he approached The Burgundy Room and noticed a huge crowd of people milling around outside, many of them extremely attractive young ladies talking into headsets and walkie-talkies. There were two Winnebago RVs parked out front and a long table piled with snacks positioned on the sidewalk. A couple of big trucks lined the streets, with a bunch of young guys in shorts and T-shirts moving equipment in and out of them.

A film shoot, Sam silently ascertained. *Cool!* He wondered if the bar was open for business or if they were using the entire place as a set for a movie. He hung around on the fringes of the film crew before he attempted to go inside. Sam glanced at the catering table and eyed a freshly opened package of Oreo cookies, wondering if he could get away with snagging a few for himself. He wondered if he could pass for a production assistant. *I knew I shouldn't have worn my flip-flops,* he thought. Still, maybe no one would notice. But before he could reach for a cookie, a voice startled him from behind.

"Sorry, bro, the food's for crew only."

Sam turned around to see a burly twenty-something guy with a goatee holding a walkie-talkie. He must have read Sam's mind.

"Oh, no, man, I wasn't going to take anything. I already ate," Sam lied, hoping his blushing wasn't too visible. "I was just admiring your fine array of delicious snack foods. My compliments to the chef."

"I'll be sure to tell him," the walkie-talkie guy answered sarcastically.

"So what's going on?" Sam asked. "Who's in the movie? Anyone famous?"

Goatee man shook his head and sighed. "Can't you people come up with an original question for once? I swear, every single person that walks by here asks that exact same thing."

"Sorry, man," Sam answered indignantly. "But the people want to know."

"It's not that kind of movie," he explained humorlessly. "It's a documentary, so you can forget about spotting Bruce Willis or Jennifer Aniston, all right?"

"All right, all right," Sam answered, raising his hands as if to surrender. He was way beyond being over Mr. Goatee's attitude, but his interest in the documentary was piqued.

Sam decided to seek out one of the more attractive, more female crew members to gather more information. He walked away from the catering table and caught up with a cute blond girl in a loose-fitting black T-shirt and khaki cargo shorts. She was holding a walkie-talkie too, but she didn't look very busy. And he hoped she'd be more friendly than the food sentry.

"Hey, can I ask you a question?" Sam asked as politely as possible.

"You just did," she answered, completely deadpan.

"Oh, I get it," Sam fired back. "You film people all think you're just too cool for the average citizen, is that it?"

He had taken enough abuse from girls this week. And while he might have expected to get some guff from the meathead by the food table, he didn't have to hear it from everyone on the crew. Sam started to walk away in a funk, but the blonde in the cargo shorts grabbed his arm.

"Hey, wait a minute," she said, suddenly flashing a big, friendly smile. "Can't you take a joke?"

Now Sam felt like the jerk. "Oh, I'm sorry. I guess I've just had a rough day."

"Yeah, I think we all have," she answered sympathetically.

"Anyway," Sam continued, relieved that he wasn't getting the cold shoulder after all. "I was about to get a beer here at The Burgundy Room when I noticed the film crew and everything. I asked Buster over there if there was anyone famous in the movie, and I guess people have been asking you guys that same thing all day, and he got a little crabby on me, but he did tell me that it's a documentary. . . ."

"So what's your question?" Cargo Shorts maintained her friendly smile, but she was obviously getting a little impatient with Sam's meandering.

"What's the documentary about?" Sam blurted out.

"It's about landmark bars and taverns that have been around for at least fifty years," she explained.

"Landmark bars, really? That is so dope!" Sam exclaimed. "And The Burgundy Room is one of them?"

"That it is," she answered, and Sam was relieved when she didn't add, "Obviously."

"So, do you come here often?" the girl asked.

"Well, yeah," Sam answered. "It's, like, my favorite bar."

"Is it really?" For a second she sounded suddenly more interested, but then she caught herself. "Or are you just saying that because you think we might put you in the movie?"

Sam couldn't believe his ears. Was it really possible that he could be in this cool documentary about landmark bars, or was this girl just messing with him?

"No, it really is my favorite bar," Sam insisted. "Why? Are you really putting customers in the movie?"

"A few," she answered. "In fact, that's one of

my jobs: to find people who would be good to talk on camera about the bar."

"Wow, that would be so righteous to be in a documentary, talking about The Burgundy Room." Sam found himself getting a little bit too excited and tried to catch himself. He wiped his sweaty hand on the side of his shorts and extended it. "By the way, my name's Sam. Sam Burgess."

The blonde reached out and shook his hand. "Sara. Sara Howe."

"Sara Howe ya doing," Sam said, realizing too late that he had just said another lame thing that hundreds of lame-os had said before him.

Luckily Sara ignored his remark. "So, Sam, why is The Burgundy Room your favorite bar?"

"Well, for one thing, it's really close to my house," he answered without thinking. *Oops!* he thought. *That's no way to get yourself in this documentary.* And before Sara could respond, he added, "And, well, it just has a lot more, like, history than all the other bars around campus."

"Wow, you really do want to be in this film, don't you?" Sara teased him.

"No," Sam protested. "I mean, yeah, I do. But it's true. This place just has way more character. And, well, it's the one place around here that isn't always packed with a bunch of college kids. I mean, there are always a few here. But you also see

31

a lot of professors and stuff. And old guys. You know, like barflies. Way more interesting than a bunch of SVUers."

"So, do you go to school here?" Sara asked.

"Oh, Lord, no. I go to OCC." For a second there Sam had forgotten about the usual consequences of admitting he went to OCC. Now he half expected Sara to turn around and walk away. *Thanks a lot, but we're, uh, looking for someone a little more collegiate for the interviews.*

But much to his surprise, his response seemed to make her even more interested. "Oh, that is so great," she said with a big grin. "You're the first person I've met today who doesn't go to this stupid school."

"Really?" Sam asked incredulously, surprised to hear another person within a two-mile radius dissing SVU.

"Yes, really," Sara answered. "So, would you like to be interviewed?"

"Yeah, definitely," Sam practically shouted.

"It might take a while," Sara cautioned. "Do you mind hanging out?"

"Not at all." Sam shrugged. "I was coming here to get a beer anyway. Is it okay if I go inside and get a drink?"

"Of course. Just make sure you give me the check when you're done so we can take care of it."

"Cool. I'll be right inside. Just let me know when you need me." Sam gave her a big smile and patted her on the side of the shoulder.

Sara smiled back and winked. "Just don't get *too* drunk, okay, Sam?"

Sam strolled into the bar with a new lease on life. Finally his day was turning around. And all because he had decided to get a beer. Now he had met a cool chick, was about to drink for free, and might even end up being in a movie.

Sam gazed around in awe as he entered The Burgundy Room. A youngish guy in jeans and an untucked oxford shirt was walking around behind the camera operators, checking out the angles and inspecting the lighting and occasionally pulling crew members aside to have a few quiet words with them. Sam guessed he was the director. Somehow he had expected an older guy in a director's chair, wearing a beret and shouting orders into a megaphone.

The whole scene was so fascinating to watch. Ernie, the grizzled old bartender, was suddenly the star of the show. A cutie with blue hair dressed in army pants and a tight T-shirt was powdering his forehead as the director guy was telling him to just act natural.

"Ernie, what's up?" Sam greeted him. "You gonna be famous or what?"

Ernie answered with his regular scowl and proceeded to pull a pint of draught beer for Sam without even asking him what he wanted. "Here you go, Sammy."

Sam took a seat at a table off to the side and watched the shoot unfold in front of him. He was taken with the entire scene. The director, calm and in control, coordinating all the crew members. Cute production assistants at his beck and call. All the lights. The cameras. The action. Sam was digging everything about it. And soon he'd be a part of it himself.

Thought-book entry (scrawled on napkin at The Burgundy Room)

Finally have an ambition for myself. An idea. A goal. A calling. Would be so cool to film my own documentary. Totally inspired by bar documentary being shot at Burgundy Room tonight. Energy is incredible. Everything about it makes me want to go into film. Documentary in particular. Forget fiction. I want to tell a story that's real. But what?

I've got it! I'll make a documentary about myself. I could call it Loser. *Totally ironic, of course. Oops. That title's already been used, and that movie sucked! Mine will be great. An exploration of my own existence. Can use my movie to show the boneheads I live with how great my life really is.*

Hanging out at landmark bars. OCC—it is a real school! All my buds. Chicks. Grappling with the whole SVU superiority complex.

This is going to be so killer. I can't wait to get started. But how?

Must go to school tomorrow and look into film classes. I hope it's not too late to add a class. Might have to drop something worthless in exchange— maybe history or bio.

Finally something to do with my life!

For once in his life Sam didn't hit the snooze button when his alarm went off. Even though he had stayed late into the night at The Burgundy Room, getting his complimentary buzz on, gearing up for his interview, totally flubbing his interview, and then hopelessly chatting up Sara until she finally made a forced reference to "my boyfriend."

Sam sprang up in bed and surveyed the mess that surrounded him. Briefs, half clean, half worn; T-shirts; socks; and worn-out pairs of his signature baggy shorts, creating a crusty top layer that obscured the wrinkled remnants of what used to be considered his "nice clothes." Here and there the neglected cuff or collar of a button-down shirt worn months ago peeked through the mess of skate wear.

Empty bags of Fritos and Doritos crinkled underfoot as he made his way across the room. Would all this mess be included in his slacker documentary? he wondered. Or would he finally clean his room before sharing his own private little world with the rest of humanity? Those questions would have to be answered later. Right now Sam needed to drive his superclean car to campus and get himself registered for a film class.

Ten minutes later Sam pulled his dilapidated car into his "secret" spot in the faculty parking lot at Orange County College and climbed out into the sunshine of another beautiful southern California day. Sam strode across campus with new purpose. Strangely, he was happy to be here, at school. He was going somewhere. He had a purpose, a mission, a destination. But his walk toward the registrar's office was not without distraction.

Now he wasn't checking out the girls just for the sake of checking out girls. He was playing the role of casting director in his mind. Wondering which of these chicks would be right for his movie. *The Sam Story,* as he was starting to refer to it inside his head. Since it was ostensibly a documentary, he had thought he'd have to know all the ladies who would be featured in the film. But now he was having second thoughts. Why limit himself? Just because he didn't know someone already didn't mean he couldn't get to know her now. There were millions of people in this world about whom Sam was completely unaware, but any one of them could enter his life in an instant and become an integral part of it in one way or another.

But it wasn't just the girls who were distracting him. Sam began to look at the physical campus in a whole new light. As he looked up through the green, leafy branches of one of the few trees that grew at OCC, he stared at the drab gray institutional building that lurked behind it, visible in the spaces between the leaves. The way the gaps in the natural living form of the tree exposed the looming man-made monstrosity behind him was suddenly a poetic vision to Sam. He started seeing things as shots rather than just things. Locations instead of places. Camera angles came to mind as he eyed the entrance to the registrar's office. And when he walked inside and entered the long, dim corridor of the first floor, he imagined a camera on a dolly in front of him, leading him to his destination, lighting the way, recording his journey.

Sam reached the add-drop desk and picked up a copy of the OCC course directory. He imagined re-creating this scene for the film. His first step toward embracing his new calling, film. This was not the moment of inspiration. That had occurred last night at The Burgundy Room. But this was his first concrete step toward translating that inspiration into reality. The camera would first focus on the stream of clueless OCC students, milling about, mindlessly leafing through their copies of the directory. None of them sure what they wanted from life or really what they were doing at college in the first place.

Fragments of conversation that had nothing to do with the future or with the world at large, giggling references to cute guys met at frat parties, would be gradually muted and the camera would silently zoom in on Sam Burgess, man of purpose. Standing alone in a sea of students. Oblivious to their meaningless lives. Clutching his own course directory with steely-eyed intention. Looking for the answer to a specific question.

There, he found it. Film Writing and Production 101. There was a section that met on Mondays and Wednesdays from 10:50 A.M. to 1:00 P.M. Two hours and ten minutes! That was a long class. But the only other section was Tuesdays and Fridays at the same time, and signing up for that one would be a clear violation of Sam's personal no-class-on-Friday rule. He'd have to drop his biology class, but so what? He could make up his science requirement another semester. Dropping bio would be a small sacrifice to make for the sake of pursuing his dream. Sam checked with the registration desk and found out that since Wednesday's class had been canceled, Monday would be the first meeting of the semester. Finally his luck was beginning to change.

Sam walked back into the sunshine, and it felt like his feet were feathers and the pavement was made of clouds. The world of OCC spun around him, waiting for him to capture it, and his place within it, on film.

"Yo, Sam!" A familiar voice broke through his cinematic daydream.

"Bugsy, what's up?" Sam reached out a fist and bumped it against the knuckles at the end of his friend's lanky arm.

"Nothing much—just making my way home in yesterday's clothes, dude," Bugsy informed him with a mischievous smile.

"Aw, dude, all right—the walk of shame. You finally got lucky, eh?" Sam playfully punched his friend on the shoulder.

"Nah, actually I was drinking beers over at Dirk's last night and fell asleep on his couch." Bugsy sighed the sigh of a guy who hadn't gotten lucky in a long, long time. "Yo, I'm surprised to see you on campus on a Friday. Actually, I'm always surprised when I see you on campus no matter what day it is. What's happening?"

"Bugsy, my boy, you are looking at the new and improved Sam Burgess," he stated proudly, sweeping his hands from his chest downward, as if he were showing off a brand-new suit.

"Well, he sort of looks like the old slacker Sam." Bugsy tilted his head inquisitively. "What? Did *you* get lucky or something? Don't tell me: You finally hooked back up with that goody two-shoes Elizabeth."

"Aw, please." Sam snorted. "That was last summer love. That was a flash in the pan. That mess is played out like suede Puma sneakers, yo. Lizzie and I are just housemates now. Strictly platonic. As in, no hanky-panky, Lanky."

"So who is it?" Bugsy asked impatiently.

"Not *who*. It's *what*," Sam answered emphatically. "Sam Burgess has a new lady in his life, and her name is Film."

"Film?" Bugsy scoffed. "What kind of name is that? It sounds more like what your last girl had covering her teeth."

"Film on her teeth, ha ha, very funny," Sam answered humorlessly. "Nah, dude, I'm talking about making movies. Yo, I am so psyched, Bugsy. It's like I finally have a calling."

"A calling? Making movies?" Bugsy raised a skeptical blond eyebrow at Sam. "Since when do you know anything about making movies? Since when do you even care about movies, dude? I thought you hated Hollywood."

"I do hate Hollywood," Sam admitted. "But that's not the kind of movies I'm talking about here. I'm talking about documentary film."

"Documentary film? Like those boring movies they show on public television?" Bugsy asked. "Now you've really lost me."

"Boring movies they show on public television," Sam repeated. "Man, you are so lowbrow sometimes. Documentary films are where it's at. Didn't you ever see *Decline of Western Civilization, Part II: The Metal Years*? Didn't you ever see *Roger & Me*? I'm not talking about fake Hollywood garbage. I'm talking about real life. Capturing one part of the world and sharing it with the rest of the world."

"Whatever, dude," Bugsy answered, indicating a total lack of interest or understanding.

"No, not *whatever, dude*," Sam fired back. "Bugsy, I'm serious. I'm really stoked about this. I just dropped bio to pick up Film Writing and Production 101. I'm gonna start making movies, man. Movies that mean something. Documentaries. Keeping it real—know what I'm saying?"

"Yeah, um, I know what you're saying, Sam," Bugsy answered in a tired voice. "And I think you're full of it."

"Dude, I am so not full of it right now," Sam insisted. "I had a life-changing experience last night."

Sam went on to tell Bugsy all about the night before. Getting dissed by his housemates and then going to The Burgundy Room. About happening upon the film shoot, meeting all the people involved, especially Sara. Getting free drinks and being interviewed for the documentary. Meeting the director and scoping out all the sweet little production assistants.

When he was finished, Bugsy finally gave him a look of recognition. "Oh, I get it now. It's all for the nookie."

"The nookie," Sam repeated, disappointed in his friend for failing to understand or appreciate the new direction his life was about to take.

"Don't you think that's a pretty elaborate scheme just to get chicks?" Bugsy challenged him.

Sam let out an exasperated sigh. "Bugsy, this is not just about picking up girls! Can't you think about just one other thing for a change?"

"Hey, man, take it easy," Bugsy protested. "You're the one who's talking about *Sara* and all the cute little production honeys. And since when is your life *not* about picking up girls?"

"Since I decided to get a life," Sam explained.

"Since last night. Since I finally found something I actually care about. Which is obviously something you don't understand."

As he ran a long hand over his bright blond buzz cut, all Bugsy could say was, "Whatever, dude."

He obviously didn't understand.

Chapter Three

Sam slammed the front door to the house behind him, strode quickly through the living room, and flung his wiry frame down to his usual place on the couch. His legs flew up, and he grasped his knees in front of his chest, rocking slightly to and fro from his momentum and newly found energy. His thoughts were buzzing, racing with ideas and images of his new film class. In his mind he switched back and forth, first to the details he recalled from the previous day's film shoot, the complexities of equipment and half-distracted people trying to distill something from their semiorganized efforts, and then to the possibilities created by his imagination for the semester's coming activities.

He saw himself first behind the camera, grimly and quietly training its glass eye on The Burgundy Room's muted interior, and then he put himself in the position of the reporter, selecting fame-hungry subjects for his probing questions, and finally he tried to imagine what he would do as the director, calling out "action" and "cut," but he found himself drawing a blank beyond that. He knew that the director was the most important person on a film shoot and was somehow in charge of the whole proceedings, but since the director neither operated the camera nor paraded in front of it, he couldn't figure out what there was for the director to be in charge of, and his imagination trailed off.

He couldn't sit on the couch any longer, and he bounded up, hands out, not knowing what to do with himself. *This'll show Neil who's a slacker anyway*, he thought, recalling his roommate's protracted teasing over Sam's purposelessness and inactivity. He became aware in a distant corner of his mind of having been ashamed of himself in front of Neil's clucking, as if somehow, since he knew that Neil—who was no snob—didn't look down on his choice of school or the way he dressed or spoke, no matter how he might roll his eyes in mock horror, and therefore might be actually unimpressed with something Sam himself might find unimpressive about himself, if he really thought about it: his refusal to find something interesting for himself to do, his willingness to let his time slough away into hours of amiable drinking and solitary thumb-numbing video adventures. His eyes cast about the room quickly, taking in the beer-can pyramid he and Bugsy had patiently assembled, which was now emitting a sour, yeasty scent, and on the floor beside it the slew of music magazines and comic books he had forbidden his roommates to touch but that lay strewn and dusty, half read and unorganized, waiting for him to get back to them "someday."

With a sudden focus of his energy Sam picked his way through the clutter into the kitchen to get a trash bag for the beer cans. *Enough of this juvenile crud,* he thought. Once in the kitchen, though, he discovered the dishes that had piled up over the previous several days' meals, plates sticky with pancake syrup, glasses coated with dried dregs of orange soda, three spoons side by side stuck to the counter, where he had placed them on three consecutive nights of gorging on pints of Ben & Jerry's after coming home late from the bar and stopping by the corner grocery to appease his postbeer munchies. The mess, which before he had ignored in blasé disinterest, now appalled and offended him. "This is what people see and think of me," he chided himself. "C'mon, Sam boy, have some self-respect."

Sam dug the pile of dishes out of the sink and arranged them carefully on the countertop. Running the water to get it hot, he sorted out the silverware and stood it like a tiny forest in one of the dirty water glasses. The sink was too dirty itself for him to wash dishes in it, so he stoppered it and squirted in a shot of dish detergent. He stood in front of it and thrummed his fingers on the chrome impatiently. He checked the water and found it was still cool to the touch. "Too slow, slow, slow!" he muttered to himself, and spun around to reach for the trash bags in the cabinet. Letting the water run, he skipped through the living room, collecting aluminum cans and miscellaneous bottles with peeled labels from beneath tables and off the arms of chairs. The fetid pyramid of cheap beer cans slid into the bag with a crash, half of them missing and rolling over the floor, releasing a little cloud of tiny insects, and he did another tour of the room to collect them all. When he satisfied himself that he had all the glass and metal trash collected, he tied the top of the bag into a knot and returned to the kitchen to stash it in the cabinet where the housemates stored their recycling before each weekly pickup.

He was just in time: The sink was seconds away from overflowing. The water was even with the shallow lip separating the sink from the counter, and merry little clouds of suds were gliding serenely across its surface like unperturbed sailboats. "Sheesh." He snorted, marveling at the stupidity of a sink that would allow itself to come so close to making a huge mess. Wisps of steam rose off the surface, forbidding Sam to touch it, let alone plunge his hand into its sweltering depths. He tried blowing on its surface like soup, carefully watching the suds boats scud away before the breeze he produced and delicately monitoring the water's ripples to make sure they didn't lap over onto the countertop. The water was still intolerably hot. Sam hopped up and down in impatience. He stared into the water with disgust, trying to make out the bottom of the sink through the murk. Finally, maneuvering two wooden spoons like salad utensils, he managed to draw the stopper up enough to let the sink begin to drain slowly, and when the water had lowered a safe distance, he was able to pull it out all the way. "C'mon, c'mon, c'mon!" he urged it. "Hurry *up!*"

He scrubbed out the sink and positioned the dirty dishes carefully, trying to get them all in so that he could soak them all at once. Squirting in a healthy dose of dish detergent, he adjusted the water to just the right temperature. Again he stood watching the sink fill for what seemed like an eternity. His mind returned to glamorous and exciting fantasies of the world of film. Images paraded before him in rapid succession. He decided what kind of sunglasses he would wear: Oakley metallic wraparounds in gold, for the "golden boy." He decided that like Adam Sandler, he would wear jeans and T-shirts on talk shows, keeping it real. He decided that he would never yell on the film set, as he had seen the producer do, unpleasantly, the day before but would maintain the respect of his cast and crew through sheer force of his talent and would garner their attention through muted whispers. He decided that he would speak only through his female assistant, a tall, leggy brunette. No, a curvy blonde. Better make that one of each. The brunette would speak for him, and the blonde would repeat in his ear in a whisper whatever his crew wanted to say to him. Or reporters. Her breath would be warm and soft. He felt himself grow very happy at the thought.

The sink seemed to Sam to be tormenting him deliberately now, its quarter-full water level rising only imperceptibly. "Screw it," he said out loud, and then continued in his mind: *Gotta go, man, gotta go—gotta get goin' and move!* Carefully turning the faucet down to a slower flow to avoid a flood, he snatched another trash bag from the cabinet and marched back into the living room, this time combing it for paper. The magazines and comic books went in a crumpled mass, and then it was stray paper towels and tissues, scrawled phone messages from weeks before, newspapers, class timetables, envelopes, unopened junk mail, and all the assorted snips and scraps that had lain out of reach or seemed like something he might get to but that now were just impediments to his new, streamlined purposefulness. Every little complicated detail had to be swept away.

Sweep! Suddenly Sam found himself disgusted by the ubiquitous dust bunnies that clung maddeningly to the scraps under chairs and the couch, and he darted to the utility closet in the front hall for the broom and dustpan. He returned to the living room step by step, sweeping wildly, puffing up little clouds of dust and dirt before him as he worked. Sweat broke out on his forehead as he stretched left and right to get every inch of the floor within the compass of his raging strokes. The pile grew slowly as he maneuvered it to the middle of the living-room floor. The air was slowly becoming veiled with the dust that rose from his wild broom strokes, and infinitesimal motes danced chaotically in the sunlight streaming through the front windows.

Sam was lost in the zone of his work until the sound of a key in the lock startled him out of his reverie. He heard Neil's cautious steps in the hall. "Hello?" Neil's voice called out mildly.

"Yo, Neil, my man," Sam sang out. "How are ya, bro?"

"Oh, hi, Sam," Neil replied. "Is Elizabeth here? I have to ask her something before—" His voice broke off as he saw Sam in the living room with the broom in his hand and a little pile of dust at his feet. "Oh, my." He gasped in mock surprise. "Sam? Is that you? Is that a broom? Be still, my heart!"

"Dude," Sam said in a tone that conveyed disapproval with forgiveness, "you guys have let this place get way out of hand on the dirt tip. Someone had to step in and take charge. Can't let the whole place slide into chaos."

Neil walked closer to his housemate, peering at him carefully, his eyes glancing from side to side to take in the half-picked-up living room. "Sam? What are you doing? Are you all right? Should I get the doctor?"

"Get real!" Sam scolded him, cocking his hip. "What's it look like I'm doing? I'm picking up the slack around here and none too late, if I do say so myself." He gave Neil a sarcastic *tsk-tsk*.

Neil retained his cautious stance and slowly circled Sam with small, suspicious steps. "You're not Sam," he charged in a soft tone. "I know Sam, and you're not him. What have you done with Sam? What have you done with my housemate?" Neil's face drew into mock horror, and his voice rose to a fevered pitch. "What have you done with Sam, you fiend? You won't get away with it! You can't take Sam away! Not unless you swear never to bring him back!"

Sam laughed at Neil's dramatic needling. He knew he had some heckling in store for his dramatic change of course, and personally he thought Neil was pretty funny. But nothing was going to slow down the new Sam with a plan and a broom in his hand.

"All right, Neil," he said with a chuckle. "Fair enough, fair enough. I guess you were kind of right with what you said before about my not doing anything." Sam paused and leaned on the broom contemplatively. "I guess things have been leaving me pretty cold lately, you know? It's been kind of hard to get excited about anything, and maybe I've been hiding out a little, waiting for something to hit me the right way. And then yesterday, when I saw that film crew outside The Burgundy Room, I felt it right here, you know?" He pointed to his chest. "That's the thing for me, man, film. It is so cool! I mean, not the whole movie-star trip and all, but just the idea of putting moving pictures down and telling a story—it's just, I don't know, interesting. Like, I had never really thought about it before, but the way they tell a story and bring it to the people, and the way it's so direct and real, you know? Not like writing or taking pictures, where you can take something just totally out of context, but when you have the whole thing, the whole scene, and the sound, it's just, I don't know, cool." Sam realized that he was blathering, but he didn't let it bother him. He was still trying to figure out in his own mind what was so interesting to him about film, and he wasn't afraid that Neil would think he was stupid for thinking out loud.

"Hmmm," Neil responded thoughtfully. "I think I see what you mean. Anyway, what's it got to do with the broom? You going to try to sweep your way into pictures? Actually, that may not be a bad idea. If you get better at sweeping first." He emitted a little cough and waved his hand through the dust swirling in front of his face.

"Yeah, well." Sam avoided his gaze sheepishly. "I guess I just have to get things together a little, you know, get organized so I can get some things done. I mean, a film has a lot of complicated details, and I'd better be able to keep track of everything. Anyway, signing up for my first film class has me really psyched, and it was about time I pitched in a little around here."

Neil smiled broadly. "Happy day, oh, happy day." He chortled. "Here, I'll hold the dustpan for you."

Just then Elizabeth's voice called out from the hallway. "This is incredible!" she said, wandering into the living room, still in the sweats and T-shirt she liked to wear when she studied. Her bath thongs flapped on the floor. "Look at you two! Who'da thunk it? This place could actually be fit for human habitation by the year 2100!"

"All right." Sam groaned. "Enough already! Don't douse my buzz!"

"Okay." Elizabeth smiled broadly. "I wouldn't think of it. So, you're taking a film class, huh?"

"Yeah." Sam nodded, aiming the dust pile carefully into the dustpan Neil held at his feet. "Film Writing and Production 101. It's the intro film course at OCC. You have to take it before they let you take anything else. I guess they show you how to work all the equipment and stuff, and I know you get to make your own film. I have a bunch of ideas about that already."

"Really?" Elizabeth asked with genuine interest. She seemed to be appraising Sam in a new light, looking out at him from under her blond bangs with skeptical approval. "Like what?"

"Well," Sam drawled, following Neil's retreating dustpan with his broom, guiding the diminishing pile of dirt, "I don't want to say too much about it yet, but I know I want to make a documentary." Really, he thought, that was all he knew, that he wanted to make a documentary. The word gave him another jolt of energy, and he maneuvered the broom head deftly back and forth at the front of the dustpan.

"About what?" Neil asked, rising to his feet and emptying the mound of fine dirt into the garbage can.

"I'm still working out the details. . . ." Sam trailed off thoughtfully. "But something real, you know, something that's not out in the open, something that'll show the people the side of things they don't know is out there, that they don't want to know is out there."

"Which people? Oh, at least the people in your intro class." Elizabeth giggled. "They'll have to watch it, like it or not, probably. Hey—I didn't know you could direct a documentary from the comfort of your own living room! Or are you planning on taking the couch with you on location?"

"I know," Neil chimed in, pointing his finger up in a parody of insight. "It's going to be a documentary about the couch. And the other side of things is the bottom of the couch. Most people don't know anything about the underside of our couch. But Sam's going to show it to the world. That's why he's sweeping up! You couldn't even see what was under the couch this morning, with all the dirt! Sam, you're a genius."

Elizabeth cracked up, and Neil laughed with her, but it was a nice kind of laugh, and Sam found himself joining in. It felt good to be talking with his roommates about something he was doing instead of something he wasn't doing.

Elizabeth stopped laughing and listened carefully. "What's that sound?" she asked, puzzled. "It sounds like a radio between the stations. Sam, is your stereo on real loud?"

"Yeah," Neil replied, "what is that? It sounds like it's coming from the kitchen."

Sam blanched, feeling his hands get cold suddenly. It wasn't static from a radio; it was water

56

flowing, a full, rich stream of water running from the kitchen sink down to the kitchen floor. *"Auggh!"* he gasped, and ran to the kitchen. A clear pool was forming at the base of the sink and spreading rapidly across the floor. The steady stream from the faucet flowed on, oblivious to Sam's dismayed protests. "No, no, no, no, no, no, no!"

He slid across the slick floor to shut it off and gazed at his feet in dismay. *Brother can't catch a break,* he thought. But then he brightened and, taking off his wet shoes, made his way confidently to the utility closet, past Elizabeth's and Neil's sniggering faces.

"It's all good, my housies," he assured them. "Sam's on point." He took the mop and bucket out of the closet and returned to the kitchen. Skating around the sodden floor, he swirled the mop vigorously, squeezing the dirty water into the bucket from time to time.

Neil and Elizabeth looked at each other, then back at Sam. He could tell Elizabeth wanted to check his temperature, make sure he wasn't suffering from a 105-degree fever.

There was a new Sammy in this house, and his housemates were just going to have to get used to him.

Sam and Elizabeth sat quietly in the newly scrubbed living room, steaming mugs of coffee in their hands, a plate of cookies and fruit on the coffee table in front of them. Elizabeth and Neil had pitched in generously to go along with Sam's cleaning frenzy, and the first floor of the house shone with an unfamiliar glow. Neil was off to his afternoon classes, and Sam, meanwhile, had managed to corral some of his energy and was trying to explain to Elizabeth the idea for his first documentary that he had come up with while washing up the last of the dishes.

"All right, check it out," he offered, holding up his hands as if to frame a theater marquee. *"Sam: Portrait of a Twenty-First-Century College Man."*

Elizabeth nodded and looked down into her coffee cup. "Okay," she said. "Go on."

"Well, that's it!" Sam looked incredulous. "Think about it, Elizabeth. This is what people don't know about, what it's like for the new independent guy. And who's in a better position to show them about it than me? I can give them, like, the inside scoop on what it means to be a college man in today's world."

"Like what?" Elizabeth giggled. "All you do is play video games and think up new ways to torture me. I don't see why anyone would want to know about that. I mean, it's not like you're going to school in Timbuktu, or like you've overcome some amazing hurdles, or like you're this incredible student or anything. What's the big deal?" Elizabeth held her hands apart in inquiry. "I mean, we all know you're a freak, but how is that going to translate to the screen?"

"Elizabeth," Sam protested, "you're missing the whole point! It's not going to be about me, exactly—it's supposed to be about any college student. Like, going to class, and hanging out with my friends, and, like, what I think about things—I'll be, like, the representative for my generation. That's the whole thing—if I were doing anything really out of the ordinary, then that would just take away from the main idea."

"But why you?" Elizabeth insisted. "What makes you such a worthy candidate for a documentary film? What would make it interesting—if you're so ordinary, which I doubt anyway?"

"Because I'm the only one who's willing to tell it like it really is," Sam asserted confidently. "I'm the one who's not going to try to hide things away or pretty it up."

"Hmmm." Elizabeth appeared thoughtful. "Well, I don't know if you can't think of something more interesting than the real story about what it's like to leave the toilet seat up in the twenty-first century."

Sam paused to give his idea a little deeper thought. He didn't mind Elizabeth's doubtful questioning; in fact, he kind of appreciated the mental workout she was giving him. A lot of girls would try to appear impressed when they weren't, Sam thought, or just change the subject. He thought—not for the first time—that it was really pretty decent to be able to have a real conversation with Elizabeth. That was something he would put into his film. Only it was too bad she had given him that shot about only wanting to torture her. In fact, he mused, Elizabeth would probably make a better subject for a documentary film than he would. She had a lot more going on. And besides, who'd want to look at his mangy mug for an hour and a half when they could be looking at the fresh-faced Wakefield twin? He looked at his reflection in the coffee and wondered whether there really was anything about himself he could make interesting on film. He was beginning to think he was going to need a new idea.

"Hey, Jessica, hi, Lila," Elizabeth called out, smiling at her sister, who was coming in the front door, followed by Princess Lila Fowler again.

Sam scowled. He wasn't too happy to see Jessica dragging in Miss Jet-Set Superstar all the time. Though he had to admit she was looking pretty hot today. In a tight, pale blue, long cotton sleeveless dress and backless high-heeled sandals, she looked glamorous and girlie. He noticed that she wore a fine silver ankle bracelet dangling with tiny bells and charms of some sort. *Cute,* he admitted reflexively. Then he noticed the glittering gold-and-diamond tennis bracelet sparkling brilliantly on her wrist. *Wouldn't want anyone important not to be able to tell you're rich,* Sam thought.

"Hii-ii," Jessica called to them. "What's going on, you guys? Hey, Elizabeth, can I use your computer to get my e—" Jessica broke off and wandered slowly into the living room. She looked around for a second and said to the ceiling, "Wow, what happened in here?"

"Sam's inspired," Elizabeth said.

"No way," Jessica replied. "Inspired to mop? Go, Sam."

"I just had to blow off a little extra steam," Sam retorted, not wanting to give Jessica a chance to say anything about his past contributions to the communal upkeep.

"You've got extra steam to blow off?" she repeated tiredly. "I wish I had some. Y'know?" she said to Lila, scrunching up her face. *"Pffft,"* she sighed. "These first-year girls just *do not* know how to listen. The whole younger generation has attention-deficit disorder." Lila winced sympathetically back at her friend. "You want something to drink?" Jessica asked.

"Um, yeah, actually," Lila muttered. Jessica

turned and walked past Elizabeth and Sam and asked absently, "How are you, Liz?"

"Great," Elizabeth said with a smile. "What have you guys been doing?"

Jessica came back from the kitchen with two glasses of grapefruit juice. "Freshman-pledge torture. Lila's kind of been a champ, though," she added, shaking her fist in a little gesture that said, "Right on!"

"Yeah, well," Lila said nonchalantly. "It's not any worse than dealing with my kid cousins. You know, it's just a matter of letting them know the difference between what makes them *good* little girls and what makes them *bad* little girls."

Jessica smiled in a similarly languorous manner. "I *know*," she drawled. "It's just that they're so slow on the uptake side that I can barely keep from tearing out my hair."

Lila rolled her eyes in agreement. She shuddered in exquisitely affected exasperation.

"Hey, sister dear," Jessica said to Elizabeth, "how about helping Lila and me put up a bunch of flyers for the Theta pledge party this Saturday?"

"Sorry," Elizabeth protested. "With the time I've been spending on my student-teaching project, it's all I can do just to keep up with classes. I'm afraid dear old Theta's going to have to get in the back of the line."

"How about you, slacker?" Jessica asked Sam

tauntingly. "You got any more of that steam you need to blow off? We have plenty of ways to use it, I can tell you."

Sam was trying to think of something snotty to say when Lila interjected unexpectedly, "Yeah, Sam. Focus some of your randomly misdirected energy for once."

"What are you talking about, Lila?" Sam challenged her.

"Your whole misspent-youth scene is just so nineties," she chided him. The twins laughed in unison.

"Like it wouldn't be so misspent if I was out putting up flyers for a sorority."

"Smart guys help out the sororities," Jessica pointed out. "Think about it."

Sam faked retching. "You'd love that, wouldn't you?" he said.

"Maybe we could use you to blow off steam in Theta house itself," Lila drawled slyly.

Sam's heart skipped a beat involuntarily. *Stop it,* he said to his chest. He couldn't think of anything to say, so he just smirked.

Lila turned to Jessica. "Couldn't we fix him up with an apron and a little white hat? Now, *that's* what I would like to see." She turned back to Sam and cocked an eyebrow. A long, brown curl fell over her eye.

"Save it for your quarterback, Cruella," Sam protested.

"You're not going to get hired as a swab boy with that attitude." Jessica frowned at him.

Sam smiled in mock indulgence. "Sorry, Theta sisters," he said to Jessica and Lila. "I'm busy."

"Doing *what?*" Jessica said accusingly.

"Making a documentary *film*," he said, sounding bored.

"Yeah, *right*," Jessica said.

"A film?" Lila asked. "About what?"

"About Elizabeth, actually," Sam said, deciding it and saying it at the same time. Yes. It was a decent idea. It would seriously improve his image in this house.

"Really?" Jessica looked at him normally. "What about her?"

"The whole teaching thing," Sam said. He had it all figured out in his mind. "Elizabeth getting to know the kids, the audience too."

"So," Lila said, "you're still going to sit around, but this time you'll have a camera in front of your face. Perfect slacker idea."

"I mean," Sam continued, "we read about kids from poor neighborhoods who go to schools that have no money, no computers, outdated books, whatever, but we just mentally file them away like everything else that doesn't affect us directly. To get their point of view would be so great! And," he added, "at least I'll be hanging out with real people."

Jessica and Lila laughed. "We're real, Sam," Lila admonished him. They started up the stairs.

Jessica turned back and gave Elizabeth and Sam a saucy wink. "Let me know if you change your mind about the maid job," she added as a parting shot.

Elizabeth sat silently until they were gone. "Wow," she said.

Sam fumed.

"So," Elizabeth said. *"Elizabeth: Portrait of a Twenty-First-Century College Film Class Documentary Subject?"*

"Yeah," he grumbled.

"You could have asked," she said patiently.

"Sorry."

They didn't say anything.

"So," Sam broke the silence. "Will you do it?" he asked.

"For real now?"

"Yeah."

"All right," she allowed. "You'll have to figure out all the details."

"I know," he said. No problem.

And the details wouldn't be a problem. Right?

Chapter Four

Sam glanced up at the clock as he walked into the large lecture hall for the first meeting of Film Writing and Production 101. It was ten forty-seven, and Sam was three minutes early. *Must be a first,* he thought, trying to remember another point in his scholastic history when he was actually on time to a class, not to mention early. About half the seats in the tiered, stadium-style room were full, and as Sam walked up the steps along the right-side aisle, he looked over his classmates, trying to get a sense of the competition. Not that this was a competition, but Sam felt that in his first film class, he somehow needed to prove himself. He wanted to be the best filmmaker in Film 101. He didn't want to be some hack making movies for the sake of being hip or because of some far-fetched dreams of becoming a big-time Hollywood power broker. Sam wanted to discover a craft that he could learn and excel in, something he could use to express himself and share things with the rest of the world. He wasn't in it for the money, and he wasn't in it for the nookie. He was in it for the art. He was in it for the It. Whatever It happened to be. Really, Sam had to admit that he knew next to nothing about film. Yet. But he was ready to learn.

He couldn't help noticing a few cuties smattered about among the poser dudes, would-be movie stars, and black-clad goth achievers. But he kept telling himself that he needed to concentrate on class, on making movies, not on making time with the ladies. Still, he selected his seat in the row directly behind a very alluring young Jewel look-alike and chose to sit a few seats to the left of her so that he might steal glances at her in case the lecture got dull. In any other class he would have sat right next to her and struck up a conversation. But right now he didn't need the distraction. Not yet anyway.

Sam slouched into his seat and watched the door to observe the rest of his classmates file into the lecture hall. It was the typical group of OCC students but with a little more emphasis on artsy intellectual and a few less dumb jock types than usual. None of the other girls who walked in struck his eye quite the same way as Jewel Junior in the row below. He glanced again at her profile. She really did look a lot like the singer, whom Sam had always enjoyed most while watching MTV with the volume muted. She had long, blond hair, slightly chubby cheeks, and a smile that was totally open yet slightly knowing, like she had a secret she was never going to share with anyone. Sam wondered what else she had in common with Jewel, like maybe she was from a small town in Alaska too. And maybe she was also a poet.

Sam's attention snapped back to the front of the room as the booming voice of the professor erupted down below. "Welcome to Film Writing and Production 101."

Sam looked down to see Professor Gus McGinnis, no doubt a failed moviemaker now forced to lecture a bunch of snot-nosed wanna-bes just so he could pay the bills. He wore oversized, black-rimmed nerd glasses and sported a goatee that belonged on someone twenty years younger. He had on faded Levi's, a tight ribbed T-shirt, and a tweed sport jacket. His whole look had casual-professor-young-coeds-wanted written all over it.

"In this course I will introduce all of you to the basics of filmmaking," McGinnis began. "You will all gain experience in writing as well as the primary elements of production, including location scouting, lighting, camera work, directing, and editing. And those are just a few of the things we'll be touching on this semester. Now, I've prepared a syllabus for the semester, copies of which should be circulating around the room now."

Sam looked to his right as a mousy girl with vintage glasses and a thrift-store T-shirt handed him a small sheaf of papers. He took one off the top and passed the rest to the slacker skate rat on his left. He glanced down at his sheet and followed along as Professor McGinnis went over the syllabus.

"Now, we all have a lot to accomplish this semester, so everybody listen up," the professor warned the class. "In this course we don't learn through books or by watching other people's movies, although you will all be expected to read and to watch movies and critique them. But ninety percent of what you learn in this class will be absorbed through *doing*. Through trial and error and trial again."

Sam nodded in recognition, pleased to be taking his first film class from someone who expected his students to work. Not that Sam's work ethic had ever truly been tested. It wasn't like he even had a work ethic up until now. But with Sam's new devotion to film, he was finally ready to start working hard.

"As you can see on the syllabus, each of you will be making three short narrative films this semester," the professor explained, adjusting his glasses on his face before he continued. "You will each be responsible for writing your own films, and later today I will break you up into five-person crews, which will work together on each crew member's first film. While you all will be expected to both write and direct your movie, you'll work in some other capacity on each of your fellow crew members' films—either as cameraperson, production coordinator, sound person, or editor. You will have the option of acting in your own movies or you can cast actors from outside the class to appear in your films."

Great! Sam thought. *I have to work on four other movies at the same time I'm working on my own? How am I going to have time for anything else?*

"As I mentioned earlier, you will write and direct your own film, but each movie will be based on a theme that I provide," Professor McGinnis explained. "These themes are all listed on the syllabus, and I expect each of you to stick to the theme. The first assignment is called 'Lockout,' and your movie should show someone being locked out of his or her house or apartment and should show how the character deals with the dilemma."

A few people in the room chuckled, but Sam wasn't smiling. Why did the professor have to assign the themes for all the movies they were going to make? And were all the themes going to be so stupid?

Sam looked down at the syllabus under assignment number one and read to himself: *"Lockout": a four-minute film that explores a character's reaction to being locked out of his or her house or apartment.*

What? Sam couldn't believe his ears or eyes. *A four-minute film about being locked out of your house? How exciting!*

Sam glanced down the syllabus at the other two assignments. The next one was called "Stood Up" and read, *A four-minute film exploring how it feels to be stood up for a date.* Suddenly Sam wasn't feeling so excited about Film Writing and Production 101. He read the third assignment, *"Accidents Happen": a four-minute film that explores an accident, any kind of accident. The film can deal with the circumstances leading up to the accident or following the accident, the accident itself, or all three.*

Jeez, Sam thought, *what's with this syllabus? And what's with McGinnis? Based on his assignments, it looks like this guy's life has consisted of a series of bad experiences that each lasted only four minutes. So why does he have to impose this crap on his students?*

Sam glanced down at Jewel, who was looking over the syllabus and smiling and nodding. He wondered if she was smiling at how stupid and pathetic the assignments were or because she thought they were genuinely funny and interesting. None of the assignments struck Sam as being even half as compelling as the idea for a documentary about Elizabeth's students. In fact, Sam thought that a documentary about his own life would be better than the professor's ideas. He just hoped that he didn't get stuck with a crew full of losers.

Man, I thought we'd never get a break! According to the clock on the wall, I've been in this class for exactly one hour, but somehow it feels like four centuries. As if it wasn't bad enough that the artsy-fartsy goatee-boy professor droned on and on about things that were already written on the papers in front of us, everybody in the class started asking idiotic questions. And the answers to half of their questions were written on the syllabus too. Don't they know that the more questions they ask, the longer we have to spend in class? I think that's how it works anyway. Well, at least I had Jewel Junior to look at. I wonder where she went during the break. Half the kids who left looked like they were jonesing for cigarettes, so I'm sure they're all out front catching a butt right now. The room is much more comfortable without them in it. But Jewel didn't look like the smoker type. She strikes me as being somehow pure, like one of those girls who considers her body to be a temple. Well, that's one temple I'd like to worship in!

The rest of these film geeks in here, I don't know. . . . What a bunch of pretentious posers! Who knew there were so many Hollywood wanna-bes at OCC? I guess they're all over LA, no matter what part of the city you're in. Do I really want to go into film after all?

What Bugsy reminded me of on Friday was totally true. I do hate Hollywood. And I guess this is one of the reasons why. A bunch of idiots who think they're so creative and that their ideas are so clever and provocative that they have to share them with the world. Sheesh! Like, look at the guy running the show, Professor McGinnis. "Lockout"? "Stood Up"? "Accidents Happen"? I'd hate to be this guy's friend. I bet that all he does—when he's not trying to pick up college girls half his age, that is—is probably whine to his pals about all the bad things that keep happening to him. I wonder how many times he's locked himself out of his house! This first assignment is probably just some lame attempt to get ideas for how to deal with it the next time he leaves his apartment without his keys. Man, I wonder how many times the guy's been stood up too. And I'm not even going to go into "Accidents Happen." I'm starting to think that signing up for this class was just a big, ugly accident itself.

But no way am I going to give up on my film career so easily. I'm not so sure how I'm going to be able to do the documentary on Elizabeth's students, though. Oh, well. I guess I'll cross that bridge when I get to it. Maybe her teacher won't even give her permission. That would get me off the hook, no problem. But I still want to make documentaries. Forget these fluffy four-minute shorts about the minor inconveniences of a failed director turned failing professor. I shouldn't diss the guy too hard, though. He did say that he expects us to work in this class, and I definitely want to work. And he said we'd learn the basics of film too, which is what I need to do. So once I've got Film 101 under my belt, I can move on to more serious projects. I guess it's just like everything else: You gotta start at the bottom. And until you got the power, you don't always get to do exactly what you want to do. You gotta listen to goons like Gus McGinnis and just go along with their little games. I just hope he doesn't stick me with four boneheads for my first film. What I really hope is that he puts this young gem who looks like Jewel in my group. That would definitely ease the pain of "Lockout."

Oh, here she comes now. And here comes the rest of the class, including the prof. He must have sneaked out to catch a smoke too. Back to you later, Thought Book, ol' buddy.

Sam was still having second thoughts about sticking it out in Film 101 when class resumed. At least little Miss Jewel was back within his line of vision, which made it increasingly difficult to pay attention to Professor McGinnis.

"Now, before I read the names of the different members of each crew, I want to explain that these groups of students were compiled at random, and there will be no changes or substitutions regarding crew membership," he explained, scanning the room as if he was expecting objections from students. "So if you're upset because your special friend isn't in your crew or because you can't stand someone who is in your crew, I'm sorry, but that's just too bad. I can't waste my time sorting out the personal preferences of my students."

God, this guy's not as cool as I thought he was going to be, Sam thought. *But wait a second. When did I ever think he was cool in the first place? Expecting students to work hard isn't exactly cool; it's just something that I thought would be good for me. But now I'm starting to think this guy is just a jerk.*

Sam glanced down at Jewel, thankful for the diversion from thinking about his profoundly uncool professor. She was doodling little flowers in the margins of her notebook. *Cute,* thought Sam. *Maybe she does write poetry.*

Sam zoned out as the professor started reading off the names of the people in each film crew but snapped to attention when he heard his own name, Sam Burgess, followed by "Chris Childress, Miguel Santana, and Leslie Raines." He hoped that either the Jewel girl was named Leslie or else her name was the one called before his name—the name he didn't hear—because he was pretty sure she wasn't a Chris or a Miguel. And he desperately wanted her on his team. She was the only girl in the class who had really caught his eye. But he decided that if she wasn't in his crew this time, well, he might just have to cast her in his movie. Yeah, she could get locked out of her dorm room and decide to go over to Sam's place for a while. Sam started setting up shots inside his head, featuring himself and Leslie alone in his bedroom. First of all, the room was now immaculately clean. An open bottle of red wine sat on his bedside table with two glasses, and some really cool music played on the stereo. There were candles everywhere, and Leslie was slowly undressing by the window.

Sam was jerked out of his cinematic fantasy as students started moving around the room. Apparently they had been instructed to split up into their respective groups. Unfortunately Sam didn't know where to go. He thought he was in group four, but he wasn't completely sure. He would have liked to ask Jewel, whose real name he hoped was Leslie, but she was already in the aisle and walking down the stairs along the side of the room. The skate rat to his left was slow to get up, so Sam caught his attention.

"Hey, dude, did you hear where group four is supposed to be?" he asked.

The skater shrugged. "I think he said down in the lower-left corner, but I'm not totally sure."

"Cool. Thanks." Sam stood up, grabbed his notebook and his book bag, and ambled over to the aisle. He began descending the stairs and noticed Leslie taking a seat in the front row, all the way to the left. Score! She really was in his group. Sam picked up his pace a little, and this time he did take the seat next to hers.

"So, is this where group four is supposed to be?" Sam asked, flashing a friendly smile but trying not to look too eager.

"I think so," Jewel replied.

"Cool. I'm Sam." He reached a hand across the seat to shake.

She said something, her name, he guessed, but he was too mesmerized by her stunning gray eyes, which appeared almost translucent as she gazed at him and shook his hand, to actually hear her respond. Her handshake was friendly but firm, not limp and uncertain like a lot of girls'. But her skin was so soft and smooth, and he liked the way her hand fit into his. He could have held it there forever. But of course he let go, after letting his touch linger, along with his eye contact, just long enough for her to know he was interested.

"Hey, what's up?" came a voice from the other side of her. "My name's Miguel." A tall, dark-haired guy with muscular arms in a blue polo shirt and crisp black chinos reached across Leslie to shake Sam's hand. He had obviously already met the girl between them.

"Hey, how ya doin', Miguel," Sam answered,

78

trying to hold his own in the midst of a crushing handshake.

A short, blond kid in a faded green T-shirt and orange surfing shorts leaned his head out from the other side of Miguel. "And I'm Michael."

"Miguel and Michael, huh?" Sam snorted. "Are you guys sure you're not the same person?"

No one laughed, not even Jewel. Someone else tapped Sam on the shoulder from the row behind them and introduced himself too. But Sam was too busy checking out Leslie Jewel's legs below her short skirt to catch his name. He glanced back and said simply, "Sam." He didn't want to have to contort his body and risk hurting his hand again for the sake of a proper introduction.

So this is my film crew? Sam thought. *Four guys and a girl? What's up with that? Well, at least the chick is the one woman in this class I've had my eye on since I walked in, so maybe it won't be so bad after all. In fact, maybe I could even get into making a four-minute movie about a locked door. As long as this honey to my left is on the inside with me and these other three bozos are locked on the outside.*

THOUGHT-BOOK ENTRY

Note to self—on way home, buy two books: An Actor Prepares, *by Konstantin Stanislavsky, and* The Complete Film Dictionary.

Here I am, still in Film 101, and just as I hoped, the Jewel look-alike is an official member of my film crew. Score! So now we're supposed to be listening to the rest of McGinnis's lecture, after our brief little get-acquainted session. But I'm having a hard time taking my eyes off this honey beside me. What was her name again? I'm pretty sure it's Leslie, but I can't be sure since her killer eyes kind of floored me when we were shaking hands. And oh, that touch. That soft, smooth angel skin. I'd like to see how the rest of it feels.

Whoops! I probably shouldn't be writing all of this when I'm sitting right next to her, but somehow it feels good to get it down on paper. Anyway, she doesn't seem like the nosy type. And besides, as long as I'm writing, I can't be staring at her at point-blank range.

All the other guys in the crew are staring at her too. Michael, Miguel, and What's-his-name. Is it Charlie? And what is her name? This is driving me crazy! I think it's Leslie, but for now I'll just call her Jewel. She totally does look just like her, only more beautiful, more innocent. I can't see any of these other guys having much of a shot at her, though. I mean, look at them, and then look at me, Thought Book. You know I'm The Man. I'm like Brad Pitt, and these three losers are like the geeks from American Pie.

So I wonder if I should try to get her to act in my movie or just work my magic behind the scenes. It would be pretty cool to write my flick with her in mind. Then I could get her to do whatever I wanted—within reason, of course. But how creative could I really get in a four-minute student film about being locked out of the house? I swear, the assignments in this class are completely wack. If they only let us use our own ideas for one of our projects, then I could still make the documentary about Elizabeth's class. I'd even limit it to four minutes if I had to. I could always make a longer version after the semester is over. Maybe it could even be like an independent-study-type project. But for now I guess I better stick to the syllabus and figure out how I can make a star out of Jewel here.

Chapter Five

Sam lay on his back at his customary corner of the couch, chewing on the black plastic cap of a new ballpoint. A wire-bound notebook lay open on his lap. On the page it was opened to, Sam had written *Lockout* four times and then *Rock Out* twice, and then in large letters he had scrawled *Red Hot Chili Peppers*. He had tried to draw a doorknob, without much success. He kept envisioning Leslie/Jewel pulling on the doorknob of the house and the door not opening, but he sure wasn't getting anywhere thinking of a story or any dialogue. He pictured the front door to the house from every possible angle. Nothing. He decided he needed to imagine the scene to music.

Sam picked out a CD by Beck and was just getting his mind into a funky groove when he was interrupted by the sound of Elizabeth's key in the front door. She bustled in busily, keys jangling, singing to herself tunelessly, shaking out her blond hair, and going through the mail. "Sam! Hi!" she said, slinging her purse over the arm of the couch and throwing the junk mail on his lap.

"Hey," Sam said, closing his notebook.

Elizabeth stood next to the speaker and listened carefully for a second. She snapped her fingers to the beat. "Cool beat," she said. A second later she shouted to him over the music: "Hey, guess what? I talked to the principal today about the documentary idea, and she was incredibly psyched about it. I couldn't believe it. She is so nice. You can basically, like, come whenever you want." She closed her eyes and nodded to the music, snapping a little break beat.

"That's really nice of them," Sam said.

"She said she thought it would be interesting for the kids," Elizabeth said. "Hey, this is loud," she shouted. "How'd it go in class anyway? How's the prof? Did you meet anybody famous? Was Gwyneth there? Just kidding. Did you get your schedule yet?"

Sam's stomach tightened, and he looked at the stereo. He had been putting off telling her that he had to make movies about dumb little stories, that he wasn't going to be able to make the documentary at all. The Doorknob That Wouldn't Turn, he thought, *instead of* Elizabeth and the Kids. He tried desultorily to figure out a way to put off telling her. And at least he wanted to make sure Jessica and Lila didn't find out. He could wait to hear their comments about the slacker's insightful film about how it *feels* to be shut out of your own house because you're so disorganized. He felt the pressure building up inside him. This was going to have to be good. But what was he going to say to Elizabeth?

"So," Elizabeth said, throwing herself down on the couch beside him. "When d'you wanna come in? Did you get the dates for your projects?" She bounced up and down on the couch enthusiastically.

"I don't know," Sam said, startled by her energy.

"Well," she said, stilling herself to look at him, "luckily for you, you have a little window to figure it out before you have to commit. The school is going to have a getting-to-know-you day tomorrow. Not for the kids to get to know the kids in other classes, but for them to meet all the grown-ups who work there or whatever, all in one day. All the people who have any business at the school are going to go around to all the classes to introduce themselves to the kids and tell them what they do. Anyone can come, really. The guy who fixes the windows is going to be there. You can come. I checked."

Tomorrow, Sam thought. There was no way he could come up with a good excuse by then to save himself the embarrassment. He decided he had to stall Elizabeth a while. He would buy himself some time by going to the school and being introduced around. That would give him the rest of the week to figure out what kind of excuse he might be able to come up with.

"You got it," he said. "I don't know when we're actually going to be able to get on location, though. I have to train my whole crew. . . ." He trailed off.

Elizabeth cocked an eyebrow at him. "How are you going to do that in an intro class?" she queried him.

Sam smiled sheepishly. "Well, we all kind of have to learn together. But when I'm the director, I have to be in charge. I'd rather have the five of us working well as a team before trying to do anything in a room full of kids." He couldn't believe himself, that he was going on this way. *Stop it!* he heard himself in his mind. *Shut up! Less you say now, the better—liar!*

"All right," she said. "I'll just tell the kids that a college student is going to come in who might make a documentary film at their school. *Might,* so they don't get too disappointed if it doesn't come off for some reason. That'll be interesting. I wonder what they think about when they see a movie anyway."

Sam smiled weakly. He was glad Elizabeth had been responsible enough to think of how to present the idea to the kids because he knew it *wasn't* going to come off. It was more considerate than he

86

had been to the kids or to her. "Yeah," he managed to say. "They need some time to practice saying 'documentary.'"

"*Dah-doo-deedee,*" Elizabeth said in baby talk, making herself laugh. "All right. This is going to be great, Sam. I mean, even if you're just learning how to work the equipment. The kids'll like having someone else hanging around, especially someone who's only a little smarter than they are." She winked at him, smiling. "Y'know, they're interested in people who are interested in them on their own terms. You're almost on their level."

"They're all smarter than me." Sam sighed. He felt like a jerk.

"Me too." Elizabeth smiled sympathetically. She actually sounded serious about it. Sam felt relieved. "Hey," she said, bounding to her feet, "I'm making myself a fruit smoothie. Want half?"

"Yeah," Sam said, following her into the kitchen. He felt slightly comforted that she was still into the documentary. Maybe he could just go into the school a couple of times and hang out with the kids, talking about movies and kids and TV and stuff. They'd probably be into it. And then he'd figure something to say to get out of bringing in the camera. Elizabeth could probably figure out a way to make a cool game for them out of it.

Everything's going to work out all right, he told

himself. *Just keep takin' care of business, man. One step at a time.*

THOUGHT-BOOK ENTRY

Well, yesterday I was king of the slackers; today I'm king of the world. And much like my predecessor, director of Titanic, *James Cameron, I am directing a lot of movies. Too many dumb movies. Still, I think this is going to work out for me.*

I can't stop thinking about the one film too many, the documentary that got snuffed by Professor Doctor Gus von Film Dork McGinnis, Ph.D., resident genius of OCC. I gotta focus on Lockout, *or he's going to think I'm a joke and I'm never going to get anywhere. The thing with Elizabeth is going to have to work itself out on the side.*

Work itself out?

On the side?

Admit it! Dude, you're toast. Burned toast. Have I mentioned that I'm totally toast? Now Elizabeth and I are going to the school she's student teaching in tomorrow *to meet the students. I should tell her the truth, but I can't—can't risk falling off the face of her earth again. I don't know why I care so much what she thinks, but I guess I do.*

I'm not the king, of anything; I'm the joker.

Maybe there's some way that I can do both. No. Well, hey, how hard can it be once you get the hang of it? Find out when I get to use the camera and stuff and can I get to LA's schools on off-hours.

I can make two movies when everyone else is making one. Why not?

Yeah, right.

Anyway, the important thing is to keep my priorities straight. Get something good for Lockout, *keep Elizabeth happy, and keep my whole life away from Jessica and her whole sick crew. Last thing I need is for the good sisters of Theta house to stick their noses in on the workings of the next Stanley Kubrick. Or whatever. Even if I'm not even the next Nobody McNobody.*

All right. Tomorrow is going to be great. I spent so much time thinking about the school, now I really am interested to see it.

(I should probably stop writing, but I'm so totally used to going on and on from writing all weekend that I don't care. Weird.)

Remember: Figure out soon what music to use for Lockout.

For most of the car ride to the school Sam tried to practice not really being there. It started by accident: The muffler on Elizabeth's Jeep was so loud that speaking was difficult. That, combined with the fact that it was eight o'clock in the morning, made him give up trying almost right away. *Good thing too*, he said to himself. *I won't run the risk of making up any more stories about what it's going to be like shooting this film I'm not even making.*

Elizabeth mostly paid attention to the road. The morning rush-hour traffic careened along the interstate south to the school. Sam wondered how she had come to pick this school, so far away. He peered glumly out the passenger-side window, amazed at the sheer number of people who managed to get up early enough every day to get their cars this far down the freeway. *Cripes,* he thought, glancing at a red-faced man whose too tight tie in his too tight shirt seemed to be choking him around the neck. The guy passed them on the right, turning to look right at them before he sped off. Elizabeth was oblivious. If she spoke, it was to talk about what was on the radio. Sam couldn't make out what she was saying, but she didn't seem to mind it if he didn't reply, so he didn't worry about it.

He thought if he could just pretend to not really be there, he wouldn't have to worry about the whole thing of getting up in front of the children. He liked kids and had always had an easy time talking to them on their own level. Elizabeth hadn't been too far off with that one. But going through the motions with the *principal* (his stomach tightened at the word, a reflex learned during many years of getting into trouble or trying not to)—in front of a room of kids was something else. If he could just forget that he was acting, it wouldn't be so hard. But that meant he had to forget himself, in a way.

Good exercise, he thought. *Today I am a camera.* He tried to catalog the passing scene. Factories. Concrete highways. Cars. More factories. He yawned and wished they had stopped for an extra coffee.

They pulled into the little gravel-paved parking lot next to the school. Grass and weeds sprouted chaotically. A small, two-story redbrick building lay tucked between an apartment building and a vacant lot. A few pieces of old iron playground equipment lurched sadly behind a gap-toothed picket fence. At the base of the monkey bars there were only rubber mats on top of the asphalt in case a kid fell. Years of play had dug a little pit in the asphalt at the foot of the slide, exposing the gray dust underneath. *Whoa,* Sam thought. *This sucks.*

He spoke quietly to Elizabeth for a moment before they walked inside. "Why don't I just observe from the back of the room, get a sense of the kids' personalities without making them feel uncomfortable or scrutinized?"

Elizabeth nodded blithely. "Sounds good!" she said. Sam wasn't sure if she was even listening to him. But right before they walked into the classroom, she touched him on the sleeve of his plaid flannel work shirt. "This is really cool," she gushed in a whisper. Sam blushed.

But no sooner had Sam taken his perch at the back of the class, as Elizabeth made her way to the teacher's desk by the window, than a little girl piped up. "Who's that strange guy?" she asked loud and clear.

Elizabeth smiled at the girl. A middle-aged woman—the class's teacher and Elizabeth's boss—looked up and noticed Sam there. She gave him a little wave.

"Anya, I'd like you to meet Sam," Elizabeth answered the little girl.

"Hi, Anya," Sam intoned.

She didn't pay any attention to him. Instead she asked Elizabeth, "But what's he doing here?"

Sam felt the eyes of the other children slowly come to rest on him. The teacher—Ms. Barton, Elizabeth had told him—just turned back to the papers lying on her desk. She didn't seem very interested.

Elizabeth's voice grew a little clearer and calmer. "Sam's a college student just like me," she said. Sam grinned at the funny way she said it. *Hey,* he thought. *I don't go to SVU. I guess she just means we both go to college.*

Anya pouted at Elizabeth. "Well," she said, "for a girl who goes to another school, you sure do hang out here a lot." Some of the other children laughed at what she said.

Elizabeth laughed, then got down to business. "Sam is interested in making a movie," she explained to the class. "He just wants to visit today to see if he can get any ideas," she added vaguely.

Another girl spoke up from behind Anya. "He should do a movie about him*self*," she said confidently.

Now the entire room was following the conversation. Ms. Barton had her hands folded on her desk and was observing impartially.

"Now, why do you think that, Therese?" Elizabeth encouraged her.

" 'Cause he's so cute, he looks like he should be on TV!" Therese replied, breaking off into a giggle on the word *TV*. The children were laughing at Sam again. Some of the boys said "ooh" insinuatingly and then made wet kissing noises in the palms of their hands. Sam felt increasingly embarrassed. Then one of the boys turned his kissing noise into a long, wet, nasty *pfffffffft* sound. Now all the children were laughing hysterically. The class seemed to be teetering on the brink of losing control entirely. Sam clung to his notebook and tried to stare at nothing. A phony smile was frozen on his face. He was being made a fool of by a room of eight-year-olds. Elizabeth and Ms. Barton made no effort to conceal their laughter either.

Ms. Barton rose to her feet and stood solidly in front of the class. A few boys tried out their own versions of every eight-year-old boy's favorite sound effects, and Ms. Barton had to clap once. Then the room quieted down pretty quickly for the most part. Sam thought she seemed to have the kids pretty well intimidated.

"Writing!" she called out in a voice that was half Mary Poppins and half traffic cop. Reaching behind her, she turned around a large, white board with a long list of common words written on it in colored markers. Then she strode among the children, placing them into their chairs here and there. When she had corralled the majority of them, she started Elizabeth on passing out sheets of loose-leaf paper and pencils. Nobody was looking at Sam anymore. A few kids were always getting up and wandering away, but they weren't too interested in him anymore. Anya and Therese were sitting beside each other, looking up expectantly at the list of words.

Writing turned out to be half an hour of copying the words on the white board. Then there was math period, and then there was a snack. Sam munched on a graham cracker. Elizabeth was pouring sour canned orange juice into little paper cups. Half of what she poured, she ended up having to clean up off the floor.

Out of the blue Ms. Barton asked Sam if he'd like to talk with the kids while they ate. Luckily he said yes without thinking because he was still pretty much concentrating on his graham cracker when Ms. Barton said, "All right, has everyone had

94

juice?" and then, over the chorus of yeses, "Then why don't we ask our visitor what he's going to be doing around the class!"

Twenty-three pairs of eight-year-old eyes turned to stare at Sam. Nobody said anything for a second.

"Well," Sam said, "um, like Elizabeth said, I'm interested in making a movie. I get to make a movie for my class at college. And so I thought that I could just come to this school and mostly just sit and watch but maybe get to talk a little with some of you too. I mean," he qualified, "if you want to. You don't have to say anything to me if you don't want."

Ms. Barton seemed satisfied. Elizabeth was too busy trying to get all the tiny paper cups into the small wastebasket to say anything. A few of the children started to wander toward the corner of the room that had a few blocks in it. It was obvious to Sam that they were used to getting to play after their snack and that they weren't going to waste any time with *him*.

"So," Sam blurted out suddenly. "What's the best thing around here?"

The children starting arguing among themselves. "The radio," one boy said plainly, as if it were too obvious to be worth mentioning. "No, no, TV's better," another boy objected. The first child looked disgusted. "Maan," he said.

A nervous-looking little girl spoke up insistently. "Naw, naw, naw, my daddy's car gots a radio in it, and it plays real loud, and he's driving me to Phoenix!" The other kids looked at her appraisingly. Sam felt lost: Was she saying her father's car was the best thing around here?

Evidently so. "He do not," the radio lover denied flatly.

That started another argument. Ms. Barton waited for a pause and asked Sam, "Do you mean right here in school?" she asked pointedly.

"Yes," Sam agreed gratefully.

That made the children pause. "Well," one of them said, "I like the juice and cookies but not the pineapple juice. That's nasty."

The girl with the father with the radio in his car appeared shy suddenly. "I like to play," she said. Some of the other children nodded in agreement. A few more of them broke off to find something more interesting to do.

"Uh," Sam said quickly, "how about the worst thing? What do you hate the most?"

The remaining children thought for a moment. A small girl with very long, straight brown braids explained how when you were on the teeter-totter with a bigger kid, they didn't have to let you down no matter what. That launched a diatribe against the bigger and older kids. All of the kids around Sam confirmed getting beaten up fairly regularly. It seemed to be a large matter of concern for them, where to stand in the playground so the bigger kids couldn't drag you off to punch you in the stomach without a teacher seeing. Where you could hide your money if you had some and you didn't want a big kid to take it from you. Which way to walk home so the big kids couldn't follow you and beat you up away from any adult eye, or worse, one of the grown-ups who lived in the neighborhood getting after you. On the whole it didn't seem like they were too safe anywhere outside the walls of the classroom.

One of the girls took offense at one of the boys saying that her older brother, who went to their school, was a dirty fighter who held kids down so he could bite them. She sneaked up behind him and kicked him right in the butt, hard. The boy howled in pain and protest, and before he had time to turn around to see his attacker, the little girl ran across the room and tried to duck behind the teacher's chair. The aggrieved boy didn't waste any time running after her. She eluded him and made her way to the door of the classroom.

"Jeanine!" Ms. Barton called out. "Stop right there!" Jeanine's hand froze on the doorknob. "We do *not* go out in the hall without permission, Jeanine," she lectured her. The little boy saw his chance to get her by the door. "Mike! Leave her alone!" Ms. Barton commanded.

Mike had no such intention, and Ms. Barton had to chase him down as he chased after Jeanine. The remains of the conversation petered out as Elizabeth assured the other children not to worry about the bigger kids or the near fight across the room. Sam felt like an idiot for starting them on the whole discussion. It *had* been pretty interesting, he thought, but he wished he'd known what it might degenerate into.

"Maybe this would be a good time for me to go," he offered.

"Um, yeah, maybe that would be a good idea," Elizabeth said. "But I'm supposed to go in twenty minutes anyway. Why don't you wait for me in the car?"

THOUGHT-BOOK ENTRY

Well, I've got a few minutes before Elizabeth comes out. I do not know what to do about this. Those kids were great—they have so much to say. But I can't film them. I have to film a stupid doorknob instead! At least Elizabeth didn't tell them they were gonna be the subject of a student film documentary. Then they'd be crushed.

But at least I don't think Elizabeth is going to be that crushed when I break it to her. It looks like she's got her hands full enough trying to keep up with those kids.

So much cooler than a doorknob. This sucks.

I wish I could just stand around and film Elizabeth. I wish I could turn invisible.

I wish I wasn't going to be late for my first film-crew meeting. I hope Elizabeth knows how to get from here to OCC!

Chapter
Six

For the third morning in a row Sam got out of bed without having to hit his snooze bar once. Monday had been the first day of film class, Tuesday was his visit to Elizabeth's school to meet with the kids, and today was, well . . . it was his third official day as Sam Burgess, filmmaker. If he was going to be making movies, he had to start making the most of his days.

Sam was also anxious to call Leslie and apologize for missing the meeting yesterday. Mostly he was sorry for having missed the chance to hang out with her and start to get to know her—and for her to get to know him. Sam hoped that none of the geeky crew members who were salivating over her on Monday had made any headway with her in his absence. But thinking back on the three of them, he wasn't too worried. Now that he thought about it, he felt bad for missing the meeting for another reason too. He had let down his crew, and he knew that he was going to need them—just like they were going to need him—if their films were going to be successful.

But really he had no choice. Things had been going so well between him and Elizabeth that he couldn't bear to cut it short. And besides, it was only one meeting, right? Sam was sure that with a phone call to Leslie, he'd be able to turn on the old Burgess charm and smooth everything out. He just hoped that she hadn't already written him off as a complete slacker.

Sam fished the crew contact sheet out of his book bag and looked for Leslie's name. There were only four names on it besides his, so it wasn't so difficult to find. The problem was, when he looked at it, a wave of uncertainty washed over him. Her name *was* Leslie, wasn't it? Yes, he was sure it was. The other names were Mike, Miguel, and Chris, three guys' names, so she had to be Leslie. But then he remembered that Leslie was sometimes used as a man's name too. And Chris could be short for Christine. So what happened to Charlie? That's who he thought the guy sitting behind him in class was: Charlie. The truth of the matter was that he hadn't been totally paying attention when either one of them told him their names. When Leslie introduced herself, he was hypnotized by those incredible gray eyes, and when Chris introduced himself, he was too busy staring at Leslie's legs. The only names he was sure of were Mike and Miguel. So what if Charlie was really Leslie and Leslie was Chris?

Sam scolded himself for getting so worked up about it. Of course Jewel was Leslie and the other dude was Chris. So he picked up the phone and quickly dialed Leslie's number before he had any more second thoughts about it.

"Hello?" It was a guy's voice, which made things even more complicated.

Sam assumed it was probably Leslie's boyfriend. Why had that thought never crossed his mind before? She was so fine, of course she had a boyfriend. And if she did, Sam didn't want the guy knowing anything about him. Just in case she might want to fool around with someone on the side, Sam didn't want to leave any clues that it might be him she was seeing on the sly. So in a combination of panic and shrewd thinking, Sam hung up the phone before he said anything. Now he just hoped that the guy wouldn't star-sixty-nine him.

Sam looked back at the contact sheet and considered the possibility that she was actually Chris after all. Nah, she was Leslie, and she had a boyfriend, and if Sam had any chance of hooking up with her, he'd have to play the role of home wrecker.

So he put Leslie and Chris out of his mind and played it safe by calling Mike.

"Hello?" This time a familiar guy's voice. No surprises.

"Hi, is this Mike?" Sam asked.

"Yeah, who's this?"

"This is Sam Burgess; I'm on your film crew?" Sam announced tentatively. "You know, from Film 101?"

"Oh, you're the guy who didn't show up at the meeting yesterday," Mike answered, sounding slightly pissed. "We thought maybe you dropped the class or something. In fact, I was supposed to call you today and give you a hard time for skipping out on us. So are you still in the class or what?"

Now Sam was the one who was pissed. What was this guy talking about? Dropping the class? Giving him a hard time? Ordinarily Sam would have told the guy to get bent. But he had to admit, he did feel bad about missing the meeting. And he didn't want to get off on a worse foot than he already had.

"Yeah, I'm still in the class," Sam answered impatiently. "And, uh, I just wanted to, you know, apologize for missing the meeting yesterday and find out if there's anything I need to know or do before class today."

"So does that mean you're actually going to be in class today?" Mike asked with an edge to his voice.

"Yeah, I'm going to be in class today," Sam answered defensively. "And you've now given me an adequately hard time about missing the meeting, okay? So is there anything I need to do for class or not?"

"Yeah, Sam, as a matter of fact, there is something you need to do for the crew," Mike answered, obviously not amused by Sam's tone.

"So are you going to tell me what that is?" Sam asked impatiently.

"Yeah, I am," Mike answered. Apparently he was still giving Sam a hard time.

"So are you going to tell me now, or should I call you back later?" Sam asked sarcastically.

"Oh, I'm going to tell you now, Sam," Mike snapped back. "I just wanted to make sure that I had given you an *adequately hard time*."

"Okay, I think you've made your point, Mike." Now Sam was really getting impatient but miraculously was able to keep his cool. "So what is it?"

"Well, we need to purchase this special camera lens," Mike explained. "And since you weren't at the meeting, we all sort of volunteered you to get it for us."

"Wait a second." Sam didn't understand what Mike was talking about. "Why do we have to buy special equipment? Doesn't the school provide everything we need?"

"Didn't you read your syllabus, Sam?" Mike asked sharply. "Each crew is responsible for purchasing one specific piece of equipment for their shoots. But don't worry; it doesn't have to come out of your pocket or anything. I mean, it does for now, but you'll get reimbursed by the school for it."

"What?" Sam couldn't believe what he was hearing. "That's the stupidest thing I've ever heard. Why do we have to buy our own equipment, especially if the school is going to pay us back anyway?"

"I know, it is pretty stupid," Mike agreed, his tone softening. "I think it's just so we can see for ourselves how expensive all this equipment is so we, like, appreciate it or something and don't just take it for granted. I think we're all supposed to go together to get it. But like I said, since you weren't at the meeting, we just volunteered you to get it on your own. Consider it a way to get back into our good graces after missing the meeting yesterday. We'll let you know if you're in when you turn up with the lens at this afternoon's meeting."

As Mike blathered on about where and when today's meeting was, Sam was really starting to regret calling Mike after all. He was almost wishing he had just left a message with Leslie's boyfriend or whoever it was who had answered the phone. And part of him still wanted to tell this guy to forget it, but instead he swallowed his pride and played along. "Okay, Mike. Just tell me what I have to get and where I need to go to get it."

"Oh, all the information is in your packet, Sam. You did get a packet, didn't you?"

"Yeah, I got the packet. Are you sure all the information is in there?" Sam asked.

"Yes," Mike answered. "It tells you the name of the store where you're supposed to get it, what kind of lens it is, and what the budget is. But just remember, we'll be able to use whatever money you don't spend on other stuff for our shoots, so try to get the cheapest one, okay?"

"Yeah, but how am I supposed to pay for it?" Sam wondered out loud.

"Just use your credit card," Mike explained, as if he were talking to a child. "Like I said, the school will totally reimburse you."

Sam let out a long sigh. "All right, man. I'll do it. But after this I definitely better be back in the good graces of the crew, whatever that means."

"Oh, don't worry, Sam," Mike reassured him. "You will be."

"Good. So I guess I'll see you guys at the meeting this afternoon." Sam paused for a moment before adding, "With the lens."

"All right, dude," Mike answered cheerfully. "Later on."

"Later." Sam hung up the phone and couldn't help feeling like he had just been played for a chump. But as long as everything was cool with the film crew—especially Leslie—he didn't mind eating a little crow.

"Sure, you *could* get the Xj6 lens, and it would work for you." The heavyset counterman at the camera shop paused for a moment and looked at the two lenses he had out on top of the glass display case between him and Sam. "I mean, it'll fit the camera you're using. But anything you end up filming with it is going to look like crap."

"Crap?" Sam repeated, for what felt like the tenth time during his discussion of these two lenses. "If it's going to look like crap, then why do they even manufacture this lens? And why do you even sell it?"

"That, my friend, is a very good question," the salesman admitted, running two thoughtful fingers over his mustache. "To be honest, I think it may be so that there's something by the same manufacturer that they can use for comparisons with the Xj7, which as I've said is without question the superior lens. And I have heard of certain, shall we say 'experimental,' filmmakers who do prefer the Xj6 for its noticeably more grainy and distorted picture."

"But aren't there any other companies that make comparable lenses?" Sam asked.

"Of course there are," the man behind the counter answered. "But they're not going to fit the camera you're using. And to tell you the truth, the Xj7 is really the best value for your money."

"But I don't have that much money," Sam complained.

"Unfortunately, son, in this business that's not usually an issue," he explained. "There are so many big budgets and so much overspending in film that cost is rarely a problem."

"Well, it is for me." Sam shook his head at this dilemma. It was either buy the inferior lens and stay within the allotted budget or spend an extra hundred dollars on the lens that actually worked.

"What did you say this lens is for again?" the salesman asked.

"It's for a film class I'm taking at OCC," Sam explained.

"Now, I just don't see why they're sending the students out to buy the equipment for this course," he answered, looking confused. "The school ought to have a special department that buys all of this stuff in large quantities. That way they get a much better price on everything."

"I thought the exact same thing," Sam offered. "Apparently they're trying to teach us kids some kind of lesson about how much this stuff all really costs."

"Well, I can certainly see that," the man responded, pursing his lips and nodding. "Film equipment certainly is expensive. And if they want you to take care of the stuff you're using, then maybe it does make sense for you to appreciate the cost of it all. But when you're working on a real movie? I guarantee, you won't care a bit about what any of this stuff costs. Like I said, film is one business where money is everything, but for equipment and most everything else they'll pay whatever price is asked. No questions."

"I guess that works out pretty well for you, then, doesn't it?" Sam quipped.

"Yes, I'd have to say it does, son, which is one reason that I really can't afford to spend much more time negotiating with you over this single lens. You understand, don't you?"

"Yes, I understand," Sam said with a sigh. But

110

he didn't feel any closer to coming to a decision. It had never occurred to him that he might have to go *over* budget. And he was afraid of letting his crew down by bringing them a piece of inferior equipment, making all of their films look bad. But he didn't have much choice. He was going to have to get the crappy lens and face the consequences.

He was just about to tell the guy his decision when the bell above the door to the shop rang, announcing the arrival of another customer. So many good-looking girls had entered the store already that Sam was now conditioned to look toward the door whenever he heard the bell. He was beginning to feel like Pavlov's dog.

But this time he recognized the girl even before she called his name.

"Hey, Sam, this is a coincidence, huh?" she called out from the entrance.

"Lila Fowler?" Sam said in disbelief. He wasn't exactly on the Rodeo Drive of Sweet Valley, and Lila rarely ventured beyond the SVU campus and the designer stores nearby except for her special shopping missions to Beverly Hills. "What are you doing in this part of town?"

"Well, I just happened to be driving by—trust me, it's a long story—and I thought I noticed your beat-up little wreck out front," she explained in one long breath. "And since I needed film anyway, I thought I'd stop in to say hi."

Sam was about to ask her what the hell she was talking about. It was strange enough that Lila would even be driving down this street, stranger still that she would actually recognize Sam's car, and it was completely unbelievable that on seeing his car, she would stop in to say hi.

But before he could ask her what was going on, the man behind the counter butted in. "So do you want the good lens, kid, or do you want the cheap one?"

"So the rumor I heard is true, huh, Sam?" Lila interrupted. "You're really making a movie, aren't you?"

"Yeah, uh . . ." Sam hesitated. All this bizarre attention from such an unexpected visitor was bewildering.

"How about making *me* the star of it, Sam? What do you say?"

"What?" Sam was about to say that the film she had heard about was a documentary, not make-believe, and even if it was a theatrical piece, he wouldn't cast Lila Fowler in his film in a million years.

But before he could say another word, Lila was brandishing her platinum Visa card and asking, "So what's it going to be, Sam? The good lens or the cheap one?"

112

"You know, Lila," Sam tried to explain. "The movie I'm making isn't really about a school. It's just a dumb short film about someone who gets locked out of their apartment."

"So, I'll star in that, then," Lila stated matter-of-factly.

As Sam looked Lila over, in her sexy Earl Jean shorts and her tight ribbed turtleneck that showed off her chest to incredible advantage, plus the black sunglasses covering half of her face, he had to admit that she looked like a movie star on a weekend.

"Lila, why do you even want to be in my little movie?" Sam asked.

"Oh, I have my reasons, Sam." Lila waved the credit card under his nose like she was tempting him with fine chocolate. "So what's it going to be? Do I pay for the lens you really want and I become the star of the movie? Or do I walk with my Visa and you buy that pathetic lens and cast someone a lot less attractive in your film?"

Without another word Sam snatched the card out of her fingers and handed it over to the man behind the counter.

THOUGHT-BOOK ENTRY

Okay, Thought Book, can you please tell me: Why is Lila Fowler starring in my movie?! All right, I know one answer to that question: She plopped down rich Daddy's platinum card and bought a very expensive camera lens for my film crew today. But why did I let her do that? I mean, I could have just gotten the cheap one; what's the big deal? So a bunch of crummy student films would have looked a little grainy and distorted—so what? What do they expect on a shoestring budget? If they wanted our work to look good, then they wouldn't be sending us out to buy our own equipment. So why did I do it? Is picture quality that important? I don't think so. And I don't think I want Lila Fowler in my movie. I don't even like to look at her in real life, so why on earth would I want to see her on a twenty-five-foot screen?

Okay, I take that back. I do like looking at her in real life. She's a total babe. She's like Alyssa Milano, but taller. It's the audio track that comes along with her that I could live without. Always putting people down and demanding whatever she wants. She gets it too. And today's little stunt at the camera shop was a case in point. At least she doesn't have theme music.

Really, though, who wouldn't want to look at Lila? She's one of the hottest girls at SVU and one of the meanest, and both things are saying a lot. I wonder if she has any acting talent at all. And for that matter, why does she even want to be in my stupid little movie? Is this some evil trick to somehow humiliate me in front of the Wakefield twins and the rest of the world? Okay, now I'm getting paranoid. But seriously, why? Does she want to get into acting that bad? If she wanted to be an actress that much, I'm sure her dad could pay her way into a few auditions, at least. Maybe she wants to do it without him, although I'm positive that he'll be the one who ends up paying for that lens.

Maybe it's all an elaborate scheme for her to hook up with me. Yeah, right! Well, all I can say is, I really do hope she can act. Because I don't want to embarrass myself with my first attempt at writing and directing, all for the price of a camera lens that in the end I don't even get to keep.

On the bright side, though, maybe having a babelicious Theta chick like Lila as my leading lady will attract the attention of some of the girls in my class, specifically one Leslie "Jewel" Raines. Girls always go for guys when they think they're getting with some other fine young tender. So maybe when she sees Lila on the set, Leslie will get with the program and ditch her boyfriend for Sam the Man. Thought Book, thanks for listening.

Sam was right on time for the film-crew meeting as he entered the drab, orange-and-yellow lounge of the OCC student center. He never liked visiting this place, mainly because it hadn't been remodeled since sometime in the early seventies, which some students might have thought was cool. But Sam wasn't into retro, unless you went back at least to the fifties and preferably the thirties, like The Burgundy Room. And he didn't much care for anyplace called a lounge that didn't serve drinks, especially if it was in something called a student center. There was nothing cool about a student center unless it was packed with good-looking female students, which this one rarely was.

But Sam was here, and he had brought the lens, and he didn't want to hear any more crap from Mike and the rest of the crew. They were all sitting around on the plastic modular chairs, waiting for him, when he walked up. He was glad he wasn't late. He was even more glad to see Leslie, sporting a tank top and tight, faded, cutoff jeans. He was digging the dressed-down look but suppressed making a crack about asking her to work on his car.

Sam greeted her first, of course. "Hey, Leslie."

Did he stutter? No. Was he looking right at her when he walked up? Yes. Did she even so much as flash a smile, let alone return the salutation? No and no. Sam was momentarily confused. What was up with that? Was he losing his touch, or were they all still mad at him for missing the meeting?

116

That Chris guy didn't seem too upset. He returned the greeting as if Sam had spoken to him. "Hey, Sam, how's it going?"

"What's up, guys." Sam tossed out a blanket greeting to the three other men on the crew.

"Well, if it isn't Sam Burgess, our long-lost crew member," Mike announced, his voice dripping with sarcasm. "So did you get the lens?"

"Yes, I got the lens," Sam answered with a sigh. "In fact, I got a really good one. And you'll be happy to know that I stayed within budget."

He neglected to explain that the reason it was within budget was that it didn't cost a thing. The new star of his movie had put it on her dad's credit card. But Sam figured that what the crew didn't know probably wouldn't hurt them.

"So, let's get down to business," Mike announced. "Now, Sam, since you missed yesterday's meeting, I guess we better bring you up to speed on everything."

"All right," Sam said evenly. He was tempted to remind Mike that since he had gotten the lens, he was hoping they wouldn't keep bringing up his missed meeting. After all, hadn't Mike promised him that running his little errand would bring him back into their good graces? But he didn't want to make a stink, especially in front of Leslie, who was already acting a little icy. And besides, he did need to catch up on what had happened yesterday.

"So, since Miguel has already written most of his script, we've decided to shoot his film first," Mike explained.

"Whoa, you've already started writing?" Sam asked in dismay.

"Yes, Sam, of course we've all started," Mike answered for Miguel as he glared at Sam from beneath his bleached blond bangs. "Including you, I hope, because we're shooting your movie second . . . that is, if it's okay with you."

Jeez, Sam thought, *for a mellow-looking surfer dude, this Mike guy is pretty uptight. But I guess someone has to take charge here because I've got my own films to worry about and I can't be the one keeping tabs on everyone else in the crew.*

"Oh, yeah, that's totally cool to shoot mine next," Sam answered, trying to sound as nonchalant as possible. "I mean, I haven't gotten very deep into the script yet, but I've been working on some great ideas."

Note to self, Sam thought. *Begin and finish script ASAP!*

"So, what's yours about, Miguel?" Sam asked, interested in getting someone's perspective on what he thought was a lame idea in the first place.

Miguel's eyes lit up when he started talking about his idea. "Oh, it's pretty funny. It's about this guy who's, like, a cat burglar, and he's been breaking into all the houses in his neighborhood. And then one night he leaves the house without his keys, so he has to break into his own house. And someone sees him and calls the police, and he ends up getting busted for all the other burglaries."

"Dude, that is totally brilliant!" Sam exclaimed. So maybe this whole lockout idea wasn't so bad after all.

"So, as I was saying," Mike continued. "We'll be shooting Miguel's film first. Sam, we want you to be the boom operator, and Miguel could also use some help in scouting locations. Chris is going to be doing sound, and Leslie and I will be trading off working the camera and handling the lighting."

At the mention of Leslie's name Sam glanced over at her, hoping to catch her eye, but she didn't even look up.

"Now, is everyone cool with their assignments?" Mike asked the group.

Everyone nodded, and Mike looked at Miguel. "How's the script coming along, dude?"

"I'm almost finished," Miguel answered with a satisfied smile.

"So I guess that does it for this meeting," Mike announced. "Unless anyone else has any questions. Sam?"

Sam didn't have any questions for the group, but he was trying to think of something he could use to start a conversation with Leslie. After all, she was sitting right next to him. Maybe something about lighting.

Sam turned to her and gently tapped her arm. "So, Leslie—"

"My name is *not* Leslie," she answered sharply. "I'm Chris, okay?"

Oops. Before Sam could recover from his bungle, Chris got up abruptly from her seat and walked away. At least now he knew why she had dissed him at the beginning of the meeting. Sam turned to the guy he had thought was Chris and looked at him expectantly.

"I'm Leslie," he answered redundantly.

Mike and Miguel both started laughing. "Real smooth, Burgess," Mike heckled him. "By the way, I'm Mike, and this is Miguel."

"Yeah, I think I got that." Sam rolled his eyes and nodded. "Thanks."

Anxious to change the subject from his faux pas, Sam turned back to Leslie, the real Leslie. "So what's your movie about?"

"I think I want to do mine about a dog who gets shut out of the house and is trying to convince his owners to let him back in," Leslie answered with a slight smile.

"Oh, that's good," Sam answered enthusiastically. "A dog. That's really good."

Sam's mind started racing, trying to think of his own interpretation of the lockout theme. Suddenly he had forgotten all about forgetting Chris's name and his thoughts were completely on film. For some reason, Leslie's idea about the dog made Sam think about the T-shirt Lila was wearing the other day: *Princess*. And suddenly he had an idea for his movie.

Chapter Seven

Wow. This is too much. I have got to figure out what I'm going to say to Elizabeth, and I've got to figure it out right away. But I should have had my script finished yesterday, and I still don't know how it's going to end.

So I get home from class, and Elizabeth has made me a cheeseburger. I don't think she's ever cooked anything for me before. The burger was pretty good, but I knew why she made it for me. She felt bad about how chaotic it was at her school, and she wants to make me feel better. Ha. If she only knew.

So I'm eating my burger, and she's all up with questions. How I'm going to interview the kids on film, how much I'm going to have to shoot before I get what I need, and a bunch of other stuff. So I'm sitting there like a jerk, playing like I don't have the slightest idea what's going on with the project. She must think I'm a moron.

The thing was, I had completely forgotten about the whole school thing. It feels like it was in a dream or something. I'm much more keyed in to the real class. I just wish I didn't have to carry on this stupid charade.

Why don't I just tell her it's not going to work; it's too complicated; the other people on my crew snuffed out the idea?

The thing is: It's a better idea for a movie. It's a real challenge. There's really something there to show. Not just a cat burglar and a dog getting locked out of their homes.

Why aren't there dog burglars? I guess dogs would make lousy burglars.

Now, there's a good idea. A dog, who's a burglar, gets locked out of his people's apartment and has to convince them to let him in without them seeing the diamonds and pearls he's stolen.

Yeah. Like that versus those kids. It's not even close.

This bites. I can't think about the movie clearly until I get out of the Elizabeth thing, and I can't figure out how to get out of the Elizabeth thing because I'm so worried about the Revenge of the Doorknob.

I really am an idiot.

Think about making both movies. The packet said we'd have all the time we needed for editing, as long as we signed up for the editing studios. I can do that. I can edit them both. Why not? It's just cutting and taping it back together, right?

People like to make everything seem so complicated. McMoron and his stupid hippie ideas. Mr. Film Equipment Expert. Like I'm supposed to know about movie-camera lenses. I'd know about them if I sold them. It's not freaking rocket science.

Locksmith gets locked out. His tools are all inside. He picks the lock with his dog's toenails.

For some reason I really want to make a movie about Elizabeth. Not Lila, and not Lila's platinum credit card.

Maybe I could get Chris to help me make the movie about Elizabeth. She'd be into that, wouldn't she? She seems like she's smart enough to see through McFuzzy's phony creativity exercises.

And if she isn't, I don't want to know about it. That would be a waste.

I wonder how Elizabeth would like me showing up at her school with Chris. Wait—why should I care about that? What do I care what Elizabeth thinks of me or whether she thinks I've got something going on with Chris? I am so not interested in Elizabeth like that!

We had our little summer fling, and that was

weird enough, but it is over. Over and out.

I have got to get my head on straight. Things cannot go on like this.

Okay: It doesn't matter what Elizabeth thinks of Chris or what Chris thinks of Elizabeth. But that's no reason for me to look like an idiot in front of either one of them. And if Lila gets in the middle of this, my ship is sunk. Lila! That demon. She's the wild card in this whole thing. I can't believe I let her in my movie. That's going to haunt me.

The crew. How am I going to get the crew to go down to the school? I can't. Maybe Chris. No, no Chris. Either way, how do I explain it to Elizabeth?

What does Elizabeth know about making movies? Nothing. Problem solved.

What if Chris tells her? I'll have to get her to keep it secret. How am I supposed to get her to do all this? Why did I call her Leslie? Stupid, stupid. Why do parents name their little boys Leslie? Don't they know that's a girl's name?

I know a guy named Courtney. A guy named Lynn too. Sheesh.

Sam's a girl's name too. Samantha. Messed up.

Concentrate, Sammy.

So now I'm going into Elizabeth's school again next week. No. I have got to get out of it before that. Before Elizabeth sets the whole thing up again. I can't handle another episode like that. Those kids are too much.

Funny, though. They all want to be funny. What happens to people so they don't want to be funny anymore? Grown-ups are so boring. They need to get locked out of their apartments for there to be any reason to look at them. Kids are always interesting. Well, almost always.

Yeah, it'd be better to film the kids. But it could never work. They would never work off a script—at least not for me. And I don't think General Barton is going to help me out on this. So I'd just have to let them do their thing and run the camera. But that would take forever. It's impossible. Even if I had enough film, which I don't. And which I can't buy any more of. It's superexpensive too.

So forget it. Lockout.

The Lockout, *starring Ooh-la-Lila Fowler. Directed by suffering Sam Burgess.*

My cinematic debut. Oh, well. Nowhere to go but up from here.

Have to work on Miguel's film all day tomorrow. Man, I better not get any more noise from Mikey Uptighty. Punk.

Maybe I can do something with that big, gross diamond bracelet of Lila's. Hard to miss it. And those big, black sunglasses, Ms. High Fashion Too Cool. As if! Wanna-be starlet gets locked out of the apartment her sugar daddy keeps her in and has to sleep on a park bench. Make Lila lie down on a cold park bench for an hour while we get the shot right. Show her that it all ain't just flashbulbs and champagne. Time to sacrifice for your art, princess!

Man, why does she want to be in my movie? I do not trust that girl. She doesn't seem too interested in acting, really. And she never wanted to hang out with me before. Slumming with the OCC Neanderthals? Trying to make someone else mad? She must have some angle. Little minx.

This is good. At least I haven't worried about the Elizabeth nonfilm for fifteen minutes. Okay. Tomorrow I break the news as cleanly as I can. Take the punch. Bite the bullet, Sammo. You still look good for trying. Maybe next term. Maybe I'll go down and play blocks or something someday anyway.

And why was Lila so ready to drop that fancy plastic? Does she think I'm going to be impressed by a stupid credit card? These SVU geniuses act like I grew up on the farm sometimes. Snobs. My parents wouldn't give Lila the time of day. I can hear my mother: "So . . . gaudy, that one."

Dude, cool it. This is not the time to start thinking about family. Too many things at once. Why is it so hard to concentrate!

At least the rest of the crew liked the good lens. I bet Mr. Mikey McMousey Uptighty Righty woulda gotten the cheap one and all our movies woulda looked like crap. That one plays it too much by the rules.

I guess Lila really kind of saved my butt. Now, if I can stop worrying about what she's up to, I'll be able finally to get serious thinking about this film!

At least I don't have to go beg drama students to act in my movie like the rest of the class. That's just another headache I don't need. Those actors are worse than the film students, the weepy little saps in their black leotards. But what if Lila's no good at this? I have to tell the crew she has acting experience so they don't find out how she really got her way into this film. Acting. Acting like a spoiled brat is about all. What does she want?

Okay. Once I get the plan together, it won't matter what she wants 'cause the part is going to be so perfect for her that she won't even have to act. Lila'll just be Lila, and nobody else can be Lila like Lila can. Lila gets locked out. Who has never been locked out of anywhere in her life. Daddy always opened the door. The first time, about the first time a spoiled, rich princess gets locked out and rained on.

I make myself feel sick sometimes. But it would make some good footage. I bet Bugsy would pay me for it. Put it on the World Wide Web too.

My mind is everywhere. It's not so hard! Four minutes of movie!

Plot: Ideas for a movie get locked out of a director's head 'cause his ears are closed so he can concentrate on writing, so instead of figuring out a movie plot, he writes on and on about women in his notebook instead of getting the ideas he's supposed to be getting.

I'll write one thing since I'm on the subject, in case I want to look back it at someday. There is no doubt left about the matter of Chris. She is one righteous babe. There, I wrote it and it still looks true. So luscious in her righteous roundness, rrrar. She's going to squirm like crazy when Lila shows up. Heh heh.

Thought Book, old buddy, you know and I know that I have nothing to worry about. It's all going to come together. I can feel it. I wish I didn't have to spend so much time figuring out how to get it together, though. My fingers are all inky, and I'm going to have to get a new notebook.

Thursday morning rolled around, and Sam was the first person to show up at Miguel's place to make the first movie of the semester. *Now, who'd have thought I'd be out here at this ungodly hour?* he grumbled to himself, squinting against the bright morning sun coming through Miguel's kitchen window. Miguel had checked out all the film equipment early that morning, but he still wasn't even set up enough to be able to tell Sam what he was going to have to set up himself. And the other three were already a few minutes late. Sam eyed Miguel's couch ruefully. If he'd known they were going to be getting a late start, he could have slept later.

Except that today he had been out of bed before his alarm went off. That was surprising, but after four days in a row keeping business hours, and after a long evening writing down his ideas and questions, he had quickly fallen into a very deep sleep and woken up just as quickly, almost jolted.

Already his mind was awake, though. First day of shooting. Miguel's film. *Watch and learn, man,* he told himself. He was glad he didn't have to be in charge. Already he could anticipate the opportunities to try to make Chris laugh when they made their inevitable first-day mistakes. *I work well when everyone else but me is nervous.* He cackled to himself, rubbing his hands. *Now the time has come to reveal these* American Pie *geeks as the pud pies that they know they are and I know they are, but Chris doesn't know they are—yet. Come to me. Come to Sammy.* He laughed to himself, thinking of himself as a moronic cartoon thirteen-year-old. *Probably about the right level,* he added in his mind as the doorbell rang and Miguel hustled to let the others in. He had lain all the equipment out on the floor of the kitchen, and as he walked past Sam on his way to the door, he said, "You're on boom, Sam. We need your long arms."

So Sam spent most of the day holding up a long pole with another long pole attached to it, the "boom," which held the microphone close enough to the actor to get the sound but up high enough that it wouldn't appear in the camera shot. Or at least that's the way it was supposed to work. Actually, it took a lot more practice than Sam expected. It wasn't just that his arms got tired, though they did. Most of it was trying to anticipate when Miguel was going to move the camera so he could move the boom without losing the sound. It wasn't easy. Miguel was kind of jumpy.

Mike was put on lights duty, and Sam got a little sadistic satisfaction watching him burn his fingers as he sweated it out on top of a ladder. Miguel had them all set up in his kitchen to get the shots of the cat burglar trying to break in through the fire escape, which went out the kitchen window. Or in this case into the kitchen window or, rather, *not* into the kitchen window—hence the story line.

Snooze. The whole thing was too disorganized and random to be really interesting. The main part, the cat burglar, was being played by a drama student Sam had seen around a few times in the

OCC cafeteria, a really skinny dude named Jeremy who looked like all his joints were too loose for his own good. It was kind of funny the way he contorted his body, trying to reach around the latch of the fire escape, though. It would have looked funny even if he hadn't been wearing the requisite black leotard. With the getup, though—skintight black Lycra from head to toe—it was all Sam could do to keep from laughing out loud sometimes. Only when he wasn't supposed to, of course. Not in the long, boring moments when Miguel was trying to figure out where to put the light meter so he could tell Mike which direction to point the light so he could burn his fingers again. It just got funny when they almost had it together and they had to *try* to be serious enough to get the shot.

Which was when Sam wanted to laugh the most. Which would make the microphone shake, let alone if he made any noise—that would get him in trouble with the Keystone Krew. Sam concentrated on Zen-ing out his mind so he could stay mellow enough to do his job without acting like a total stiff, like the other four—Mike, Miguel, the actor dude, who swore his name was London (*Yeah, right,* Sam thought), and the other guy from their group, the kind of sullen, quiet one, the unfortunate Leslie.

Leslie was the camera operator, so he spent most of his time with his eye glued to the viewfinder. He almost seemed invisible. Mike snarled and whined alternately about the problems with the lights; now Sam understood why they'd be trading turns at their responsibilities. The actors who played the police—an implausible pair of first-year students in Birkenstock sandals who could have been brother and sister—stood around smoking and arguing over whether Nicolas Cage was a genius or a phony.

Chris, however, was on sound. That meant she had to monitor the recording equipment, and she and Sam had to work in tandem. Miguel would say, "Camera," and then when the film was rolling up to speed, Leslie would say, "Speed," and then when the sound registered on the meters on the recording device, Chris was supposed to say, "Sound." That was Sam's cue to get the mike in place. He wished he could have talked to Leslie enough to see how the shot was going to be framed so the mike wouldn't suddenly bob in at the top, but Leslie wasn't really into talking, and he wouldn't let anyone else look in the camera, so Sam had to concentrate pretty hard. He was intent on not messing up. The whole thing was hard enough to get going without a mistake as it was.

Part of the problem was Chris's inexperience

with analog sound recording. It was pretty clear to Sam that she had never made mixed tapes on cassettes. *It's so simple,* he said to himself, trying not to squirm as Chris forgot to say "speed" for the third time in a row and the actor lost his concentration. He looked whiny, like he wanted his juice and cookies pretty soon.

Sam realized that Chris was just missing it when the needles on the meters jumped, ever so briefly, at Leslie's word, "speed," or whatever the first sound was to register on the equipment. It was like she thought that once a sound was made, the meters would stay up in the range of the dial that showed the machine was recording. *I guess she just needs a little practice,* he thought. *It's easy enough to miss.*

So Sam ended up watching the meters over Chris's shoulder and giving her a little nudge with his knee when she was supposed to say "speed." Once she said it, he would turn to place the microphone. It was pretty easy. He could have done both jobs.

Chris relaxed considerably when she realized that Sam was going to give her the signal and that he wasn't going to reveal to anyone else he was doing it. She hunkered down and watched the comedy of errors unfold. Sam was glad to see her laughing silently at the same things he thought were funny. She certainly looked cute enough to make it fun to watch her. He couldn't make out her face, which she kept glued to the meters during each scene, making sure that the sound levels were high enough to register but not so loud as to cause distortion. (Sam could tell that she needed a little more practice doing that too, not that it was any different in principle from watching the levels on a cassette deck.) But Sam liked the graceful way she crouched over the equipment without just sitting on the floor. And he liked the way her thin, clingy, gray knit shirt clung to her torso above her short, flared, black rayon skirt and black stockings too. No doubt about it, he decided happily, this was a capital-C cutie. Curvy, but in all the right places. He considered how harsh it would have been to have to work with Mike or Leslie and thanked his lucky stars for Chris.

After a couple of hours the team started working together more smoothly. Chris got the hang of the sound recorder, but soon they were shooting the exterior scenes of the police pursuing the cat burglar. Miguel had them shooting out on the fire escape and then down on the ground in the courtyard and finally up on the roof. Several times Sam was required to angle the mike in a difficult way, and it was his turn to be grateful for Chris, who was very helpful in getting him set up in a way that would get him close enough without falling off the roof and breaking his neck. Working together with the crew was turning out to be kind of fun.

But when she started directing Sam to lean against her to crane the mike way overhead so that he could reach to his full height with her propping him up, Sam decided that working on this crew might well turn out to be the best part of this class—or maybe of any class he'd ever taken. First he just rested his elbow on her shoulder for stability. Then she was holding him around the waist, with him half on the fire escape, holding him tightly so he wouldn't fall. Her body was warm against his back where they pressed together.

Finally she was holding the boom together with him entirely, their hands wrapped around each other's, not bothering to check how exactly they were going to have to drape his body over hers to get the shot, or for how long they were going to have to lean together, or in what position. Or what it might look like to an onlooker who didn't know were working together on a movie. Sam found himself getting progressively more distracted from the actual requirements of operating the boom mike. He couldn't help but wonder if Chris was thinking the same thing. A couple of times he thought she might have chosen a more awkward position on purpose so that they could get smushed together in a new place.

Not that he was complaining. *Cute and needs me*, he thought happily. *I* like *that in a woman*.

<small>THOUGHT-BOOK ENTRY</small>

Well, Thoughty Booky, if there were any question still over whether film is the right thing for me, it's gone now. Elizabeth is being nice to me, Lila is buying me expensive camera equipment, and now Chris is bumping up against me during filming. No: not bumping. Checking me out. No: groping me. Whoohoo! Bugsy was right: Being a filmmaker is definitely the way to meet women.

This is the coolest thing I have ever done in my life.

The next morning they had to shoot the second part of Miguel's film, the heist scene. The crew of five had definitely settled into a dysfunctional family. Miguel and the cat-burglar actor started arguing right away over what the best way was for him to break in, leaving the rest of them with nothing to do most of the time but wait. Mike seemed happier on his ladder perch, rubbing his eyes and making caustic comments, and he mostly took Miguel's side, snapping impatiently at the actor guy with the double-jointed knees, who was now asking to be called Mr. X. "No, dude," he said. "You don't understand. It won't work. Think of the lighting. Dude. Mr. X. Miguel, tell him."

"I know," Miguel would cajole his actor friend. He couldn't really make him do it any way he didn't want to. For friends, the two of them didn't seem to be on very good terms. Sam imagined they probably argued a lot over whatever they did.

The scene was set on the stately campus of Sweet Valley University itself, in a random corner outside a classroom building. It was pretty out of the way, but still, plenty of passersby took a few moments to see what they were doing. *It's like trying to hang out in a mall*, Sam thought. *I wish we could be making balloon animals for them or give them cotton candy or something. Hi, kids! Do you like to look at film-class geeks trying to shoot stupid movies? Do you wanna be like me and dither your life away? Hey, you, Junior! What you lookin' at? Yeah, you. Go to class.* From behind his new, cheap plastic, yellow wraparound sunglasses he kept a rude inner monologue going as he watched SVU students watching them.

Sam kept a wary eye out for any of the Wakefield twins' legions of friends, the cookie-cutter jocks and cheerleaders who showed up at their parties and were always shocked and offended when Sam couldn't remember their names. He never remembered meeting any of them until after the first two or three times. At first Sam had been embarrassed, but eventually he decided that they were more shocked than irritated, really—like they couldn't believe anyone could not remember meeting them. The problem wasn't that he wasn't paying attention, but that they all actually looked pretty much the same to him. History major/swimmer, economics/tennis, poli sci/baseball. They all blurred together, and he didn't associate one detail, like a name, with one person rather than another. George? Steve? Who's who? So he didn't want any of them coming up to say hi and see what they were doing.

And he didn't want the twins there either because he didn't want the distraction. No, that wasn't it, he decided. Actually, he was kind of embarrassed at how lame their project seemed now, the little details that were so hard to work out and the generally ragged appearance that they had. It was more like they were arguing over which way to drive across town than they were putting their heads together to come up with an artistic exercise that they could be done with to see what they could learn. Miguel was already going to have plenty of time before him to edit it, and Sam thought he had more important things to worry about than whether Mr. X's arm was going to be inside or outside the window frame before he dropped to the floor. Mr. X was turning into a pain. *Well, you brought him along,* Sam thought.

Luckily Chris was bored too, and now that she had gotten used to the recording system, Sam was only too glad to switch off with her so she could practice holding the boom. She was happy to learn that the boom extended outward far enough that it didn't really matter that she was a little short. She held her hands over her head happily and practiced balancing the pole. She turned gracefully in roomy, faded overalls over a simple, soft white, cotton long-sleeved tee. She was better at the boom, it turned out, steadier than Sam was. She would just stand there with the mike and not worry at all about how long it was taking or whether she had the mike in the camera shot.

Sam was pretty much just left to stand there and say, "Sound." He felt pretty unimportant. *College schmollege,* he thought. But it gave him a chance to hang around her, just naturally, and the two of them formed a little unit away from the discussion over the film. They didn't talk much but occasionally shot each other exasperated looks over the mishaps and disagreements. It was easy just to be there together. Chris was turning out to be as down-to-earth as Sam had hoped.

After about an hour of hurry up and wait, they started on the last shot, which showed the burglar cackling maniacally, running his pilfered booty from hand to hand.

"Sam," Chris commanded casually. "Help me with this, wouldja?" The boom quivered awkwardly in her hands. *Must be tired,* Sam thought. He stood behind her and clasped the thin pole a little above her hands.

"Okay," she said, "now let's back up a little." They stepped backward together carefully. The light, warm smell of Chris's hair stole up Sam's nose. He tried to focus on the shoot, but he couldn't get his attention past her closeness. *If I just leaned over a few inches,* he thought matter-of-factly, *I could kiss her neck.* With effort he tried to get control over his thoughts.

"Camera," Miguel intoned coolly.

"Speed," Leslie repeated.

"Sound," Sam said without looking at the meters. He didn't want to interrupt his covert interlude with Chris. She nestled herself closer against him as she turned the boom toward the actor. Sam's arm rested gently on her waist, snuggling lightly against the soft white cotton of her T-shirt just below the frayed denim opening at the side of her overalls. He could feel the connection between them, and he was sure it wasn't his imagination.

This is better than slow dancing, he admitted to himself a little guiltily.

Sam's reverie was interrupted by his name called out in a loud voice. "Sam! Oh my God! What are *you* doing here?"

He jerked up: It was Lila! *Horrors*, he thought. She was walking toward the crew, waving at Sam. She was dressed in head-to-toe white and shone in the noon light with an unearthly glow. Bright highlights came from her dazzling white smile. The entire crew turned to look at her. It was impossible not to: with her glossy chestnut hair set against all that white, she stood out instantly, as she obviously preferred to do. "Oh my God!" she repeated. "Is this, like, your film group?"

Mr. X threw up his hands in despair. "Oh, perfect, just perfect—this is just *not* what I needed. Who *is* this person?"

"Cut," Miguel said finally. "Um, Sam?" Everyone turned to look at him now. Chris detached herself from him and turned to face him curiously.

Sam turned over the boom to Chris. "Uh, sorry, everyone. Lila, we were shooting a scene!"

"Oh, no!" Lila exclaimed. "And I ruined it. I'm sorry—I didn't know! Gosh, I guess I'd better learn a little about this stuff before I start our movie!"

The rest of the crew was looking back and forth between Lila and Sam. "Um, everyone, this is Lila. Lila, everyone. Ah, I'm going to use Lila in my lockout movie. She's, like, an aspiring actress."

"Hi," Chris said. "I'm Chris."

Lila ignored her. "So, Sam," she said. "When do *we* start filming?"

"Um, day after tomorrow, I think, if we can ever get this one finished. Look, Lila, could we talk about this later? We were really almost done here."

"Oh, I'm sorry," Lila apologized again. "So, when do I get my script anyway? I really need to rehearse. Can you come by Theta house tonight so we can go over it together?"

"Actually, it's not quite ready yet, Lila. I'll call you as soon as I get home. I promise, all right?"

"Fine," Lila said. She peered a little more closely at Leslie behind the camera. Leslie bridled territorially, shielding the viewfinder from her view. Lila laughed and turned to Sam. "This is too much, Sam," she scolded him. Her voice sounded like an exaggeration of a pop princess, but Sam knew that she wasn't usually too careful about distinguishing between *pretending* to be a princess and acting like she actually *was* one somewhere. He could tell that she was enjoying the attention and wondered if Chris could take over the boom work for the last shot so that he could get Lila out of all of their hair. She was looking shyly but patiently at the toes of her sneakers.

"I know," Sam said, "why don't you just watch us shoot this scene from over there so we can get it done, and then maybe we can get lunch and brainstorm? I'd like to bounce a couple of ideas off you."

Lila paused as if to consider her schedule. "Well, tonight would be better," she drawled.

Mike coughed into his hand. "Hey, Burgess, you want to take your starlet to the casting couch later so we can finish up with our *work* here?"

Sam flushed deep crimson. Was there no way he could get out of this without getting embarrassed any further? Lila took a deep breath and paused to look around the crew more closely. Turning to Mike, she said, "I'm sorry, I didn't get your name." He started to blurt something out, but she silenced him with a single hand raised palm out. And then, without waiting for him to answer, she turned back to Sam. "Can't you all use a break anyway?"

Chris sighed and laid the boom down on the grass. She looked at Lila with a look of wonder on her face, as if Lila had just been revealed as coming from outer space. Lila returned Chris's gaze as if she had just noticed her for the first time. Then

Lila turned away as if Chris had snot running out of her nose or something. Sam cringed inwardly. *Oh, this is just going to be too much,* he thought. "Look," he said mildly, "I'll do whatever you want. Just let us get this finished, wouldja, Li?"

Lila nodded briskly as if she had just heard her number called at bingo. "Theta house," she informed Sam, pointing lankly at his chest. "Eightish. No, tenish. Wait, I'll call you and leave you a message. I have to talk to Jessica again tonight anyway."

Sam didn't say anything but nodded. He didn't want to drag it out any further.

"Don't blow it," she added. "An actor prepares, you know." Recognizing the title of Konstantin Stanislavsky's classic work on acting, the very book he had been reviewing over the past few days, Sam was confused, and then impressed, and then he realized that she was belatedly trying to make a joke out of how long she was making everyone wait for her.

Just what this one needs is another reason to think she's the center of the world. Lila waved to the whole little group again gaily, as if they had all come to visit her instead of her having interrupted them. "Nice meeting you all!" she chirped, and Sam was surprised to see that Miguel and Leslie actually waved back and Miguel thanked her, for no apparent reason. *She just has that effect on them,*

146

Sam considered ruefully. Lila swished away down the winding brick path, reaching immediately for the slim cell phone in the pocket of her blazer.

"All right," Miguel said, seemingly calmed by the experience. "Let's try that one more time."

Sam switched back to watching the meters on the recorder and was pleasantly surprised that Chris looked back at him for more help with the boom. He tried to get back to the position they were in before Lila barged in, but there was no re-creating that moment. No denying it—it was going to be a little uncomfortable this time. Turning his head back to the recorder for what he hoped was the last time, he reflected again on Lila's lame little joke. Well, at least she knew about Stanislavsky, he decided. *I didn't know her interests went beyond money and men,* he thought. *I wonder what else I might not know?*

"Speed," he heard just in time.

"Sound!" he uttered reflexively. Chris turned again, twisting the boom to follow London again. Her hair brushed against Sam's neck, and he smiled.

Chapter Eight

Sam was feeling good. He was back in The Burgundy Room, where it all began. The original film crew was long gone from the bar, but now Sam was enjoying the company of another film crew, or at least his one favorite member of it. Cute Chris Childress was sitting across from him in the dimly lit booth, two frosty brews standing on the table between them.

"I gotta say, it just doesn't get much better than this," Sam said as he stretched his arms out to his sides and gazed into Chris's eyes.

"What, are we suddenly in a beer commercial now?" Chris answered playfully.

Sam was somewhat taken aback. It was the first sassy remark she had made since he'd met her. All day on the film set she had been so sweet and deferential, always laughing at Sam's

149

jokes but never cracking any of her own.

"No, but we should be," Sam answered, realizing how trite his statement had sounded and now trying to suavely overcome it. "I mean, look at this—enjoying a tasty pale ale, two attractive, up-and-coming filmmakers, relaxing in each other's company after a long day on set. If they filmed us right now, they'd sell tons of beer, and it wouldn't matter how it tasted."

Chris took another sip from her pint glass. "I have to admit, this beer does taste pretty good."

"Yeah, it does," Sam agreed. "So you like ale, huh?"

"Oh, yeah," Chris answered with enthusiasm. "My two favorite beers are India pale ale and stout."

"Stout, huh?" Again Sam was surprised. "Somehow I didn't peg you for a stout drinker."

"Oh, I love it, especially when it's dark," Chris answered, licking her lips.

"Wow, you're a girl after my own heart." Sam took another tug on his brew. "You're beautiful, interested in film, *and* you like beer."

"What's that old saying?" Chris asked. "'Flattery will get you everywhere'?"

Sam chuckled. "I think it's 'flattery will get you nowhere,' but I like your version better."

"Yeah, well, keep talking." Chris smiled her

sweet Jewel smile and took another sip from her frothy beer.

"So did I tell you that this is the place where I first decided I wanted to go into film?" Sam asked.

"Yeah, I think so," Chris answered uncertainly. "Something about a documentary?"

"Right." Sam shifted in his seat. He didn't like to repeat stories he had already told, but being in The Burgundy Room, it was hard not to relive that fateful night from the week before. "They were filming a documentary about landmark bars, and I basically just walked right into it."

"Sounds like fate," Chris answered, lacking any hint of sarcasm in her voice.

"Yeah, I think it was." Sam smiled and stopped talking. For now he was happy just to look across the table at Chris and appreciate the soft, smooth contours of her cute little face. But every time he tried to lose himself in the moment of her easygoing company, Lila Fowler's she-devil facade would flash before his eyes. Sam knew he was better off with sweet, no-stress, beer-loving Chris, even if she wasn't the brightest bulb on the Christmas tree. But for some reason he couldn't get Lila out of his mind.

Sam thought back to earlier in the day when Lila had walked onto the set. He had been so struck by her reference to Stanislavsky, the book

Sam had been reading to familiarize himself with the acting process. Now he wondered if Chris had been reading the book too. After all, Professor McGinnis had suggested that everyone in the class get a copy. Maybe they could get beyond the discussion of beer and talk about something meaningful that related to film.

"So, have you picked up that Stanislavsky book yet?" Sam asked pointedly.

A blank look overtook Chris's face. "Stan *who?*"

"Stanislavsky," Sam repeated. "As in, *An Actor Prepares*, by Konstantin Stanislavsky?"

Chris flashed another puzzled look. "Never heard of it."

"Of course you have," Sam answered. "McGinnis brought it up on the first day of class."

"And it's a *book?*" Chris asked, as if she were new to the concept of the written word.

"Yes, it's a book." Sam could hear the growing impatience in his own voice. "It's only the most important text ever written about the actor's craft. Well, anyway, it's really good. You should get a copy, especially if you're going to be doing any acting."

"Yeah, um, I'm not that interested in acting, really," Chris explained. "I think I want to just direct."

"Well, part of directing is telling your actors what to do, isn't it?" Sam asked rhetorically.

"I guess so," Chris answered uncertainly.

Sam raised his eyebrows. "So, don't you think you should know something about acting, then?"

"Oh. Yeah." Chris sounded like she had just been struck by a revelation. "That's a good point."

For a second Sam was dumbstruck. He wasn't quite sure how to proceed with the conversation anymore. He supposed he should stick to basic stuff, like beer, and maybe pretzels or something. *So, do you like pretzel rods or the curly kind?* he asked inside his head.

Luckily Chris provided him with a respite. "I think I need to go to the ladies' room, if you'll excuse me," she mentioned sweetly.

"Oh, no problem. Of course."

Chris got up from the table, and Sam breathed a sigh of relief. He wished he had brought along his journal. Since he had discovered his new interest in film, he had been writing in it more than ever. But right now the trusty thought book was back at the house, so he had to settle for recording his thoughts on a bar napkin.

THOUGHT-BOOK ENTRY *(scrawled on napkin at The Burgundy Room)*

"Stan who?" she asks! How can this girl call her-self a film student when she's never even heard of Stanislavsky? I mean, I've only been really inter-ested in film for one week, and I knew who Stan the Man was since before I was born. Sheesh! Even Lila "Shop-Till-You-Puke" Fowler knows Stan the Actin' Man.

I guess there's a reason why this girl goes to OCC, and it happens to be another three-letter word: d-u-m.

But still, she's so cute and sweet and easy to talk to. She likes beer, and, and . . . did I mention how cute she is? So how come every time I stare into her eyes, Lila Fowler's evil smile pops up? This is so weird; it's like she's haunting me like some kind of wicked witch. Well, at least she doesn't have a big wart on her nose. And at least she knows something about acting after all. Unfortunately, I know she's nothing but trouble. So why can't I just be happy with cute, beer-loving, no-problem Chris? Who cares if she's a dimwit? That's never stopped me before!

No sooner had Chris returned to the table than Sam was surrounded by a gaggle of giggles and two familiar voices calling his name. He looked up to see Jessica and Lila and a bunch of their Theta sis-ters filling up the previously quiet confines of

The Burgundy Room. Yes, Lila was definitely haunting him.

"Hello, Sam," Jessica cooed, glancing suggestively from him to Chris across the table. "Well, well, well. Who's your friend?"

Sam was hoping his flushed face wasn't too evident in the candlelight. "Hi, Jessica," he greeted her begrudgingly. "Um, this is a friend of mine from film class, Chris Childress. She's also on my film crew. Chris, this is Jessica Wakefield, one of my housemates."

Jessica reached out and politely shook Chris's hand. "Nice to meet you, Chris. I'm so sorry to see you stuck here with Sam Burgess. But I guess if you two are working together, then spending time together can't exactly be avoided. But as someone forced to share the same house with him, please allow me to extend my deepest sympathies."

"Um, thanks, I guess," Chris answered uncertainly.

"Hello, Mr. Director." Lila leaned in across the table and planted a big, wet kiss on Sam's cheek. Then she stood up straight to smooth her tight skirt over her thighs and flashed Chris a catty look. She cleared her throat impatiently.

"Oh, and Chris," Sam added, wiping his cheek with his hand, "this is Lila Fowler. She's going to be acting in my film."

"We met earlier," Lila coldly reminded him, offering the slightest nod toward Chris.

Chris smiled coolly and nodded back in Lila's general direction. The tension between them was palpable.

Sam shook his head in disbelief as he looked up at Lila, standing above their booth. There's no way he could be attracted to rich-princess Lila Fowler. No matter how great she looked tonight. Girls like her totally made Sam sick. So why couldn't he keep his eyes off her, especially when nice, sweet, cute Chris was sitting right across from him?

Jessica drifted off toward the bar, but Lila remained standing menacingly above the table. Sam realized he needed to say something to get rid of her. "So, uh, what are all you Theta girls doing at a respectable place like this?"

"Respectable," Lila repeated. "Very funny. Why, we're here to dance, of course. Why else would a hot group of girls like this be out on the town?"

"So why didn't you guys go to Starlights or at least somewhere where they actually have a dance floor?" Sam asked.

"Starlights is so *over*, Sam. There's always some lame band playing there," Lila answered defiantly. "Besides, we like the ambience here. And who needs a dance floor when we can make our own?"

"Make your own?" Sam said dubiously.

"Oh, just watch us, Sam," Lila fired back. "Watch and learn."

And with that she snapped her fingers, and at least three Theta sisters gathered around her. "Girls, give me a hand moving some of these tables. Come on, let's go!" she ordered.

And like a small SWAT team of scantily clad hotties, Lila and her minions set about clearing a section of The Burgundy Room for their own personal disco. Sam watched in awe as Lila made her way to the DJ, who was spinning mellow swing tunes. She whispered something in his ear, and when the song ended, a vibrant drum-and-bass track came on the sound system. Suddenly the area that had been cleared of tables was filled with half a dozen Thetas shaking their bodies to the music.

It was like Lila had single-handedly taken over the bar and converted it into her own pleasure palace. And even though Sam wasn't a big fan of drum and bass, he had to respect what Lila had just accomplished, all in a matter of minutes.

Maybe that was why he kept feeling himself inextricably attracted to Lila Fowler: Whenever she wanted something done, she did whatever was necessary to make it happen. She wasn't like sweet, quiet Chris, who always followed the rules.

Lila made her own rules. She wanted to be in Sam's film, and now she was. She wanted to dance at The Burgundy Room, and suddenly it felt like a dance club, with her and all her friends controlling the space.

At first Sam had thought that Lila's money was the thing that allowed her to get whatever she wanted. But now he wasn't so sure. Money was definitely part of it. But now it looked like it was her own moxie—even more than money—that made her capable of doing and getting whatever she wanted whenever she wanted.

"Uh, Sam?" Chris asked tentatively over the music from across the table, suddenly bringing his attention back to the not-so-quiet booth. "I should probably be going soon."

"Oh, really?" Sam answered, disappointment ringing in his voice. Hearing himself speak, he wondered if he was more disappointed that his date with Chris was coming to an end or that he'd have to miss out on watching Lila and her Theta dance party tearing up his favorite bar. "But it's not even midnight yet. Don't you want to stick around for one more beer?"

"No, I really need to get home to bed. You know, big day tomorrow and everything—but you can stay if you want, I mean, now that your *friends* are all here. I can just call a cab or something."

"Oh, don't be silly, Chris. Of course I'll drive you home," Sam insisted. "So, if you're ready, let's go."

Chris got up from the table, and Sam followed her across the makeshift dance floor. He nodded and smiled coolly as he passed Jessica and Lila dancing together. And as soon as he was by them, he could feel a manicured finger digging into his posterior. He practically jumped into the air in surprise. His butt. Had just. Been pinched. Sam shot a shocked glance over his shoulder and saw Lila smiling wickedly as Jessica was holding her side, laughing. Sam didn't miss a step, hurriedly following Chris out the door and into the relative safety of the night.

THOUGHT-BOOK ENTRY

Thought Book, old buddy, you're never going to believe this, but Lila Fowler pinched my butt! *No girl has ever done that to me before, I swear. God, it made me feel like a piece of meat. Or worse, like some piece of her daddy's property. How could I have ever been attracted to that she-devil for even a minute?!*

Okay, get ahold of yourself, Sammy. Admit it: You still are attracted to her. And that little pinch only heightened the attraction. It's not the same as when a guy pinches a girl's butt. That's disgusting,

159

an absolute no-no. Sexual harassment and all of that. But a girl pinching a guy? Somehow that's different. I'm not saying it's okay. Oh, no, she was totally out of line. But I can't help it. It was kind of exciting. It was, I don't know . . . titillating. My blood totally rushed to my head. And when I got outside The Burgundy Room with Chris, it was like I had lost all interest in her. I wanted to be back inside with Lila and all of her disgustingly beautiful, stuck-up, babelicious fiends, I mean friends. No, I mean fiends. Like I said before, that girl is nothing but trouble. And now I'm stuck with her starring in my movie.

Which reminds me: At least something good came of that pinch. And in fact, maybe it was just the thing I needed to get myself going on this script. Because as soon as I got home from dropping off Chris (quick smooch on the lips—no big deal . . . like I said, after that pinch my mind was elsewhere), I sat right down and started writing. And even if I do say so myself, my concept for the film is rather brilliant. And here's the beauty of it: I wrote it totally with Lila Fowler in mind. It's like a special tribute—or send-up is more like it—of the star. So here it is in a nutshell:

Rich princess locks herself out of her apartment. And the girl is so wealthy and cares so absolutely nothing about where her money even comes from—

her billionaire father, of course—that instead of call-ing a locksmith, she decides to simply buy a brand-new house and replace each and every one of her possessions. Her car keys were inside too, so she just buys herself a new car as well.

Oh my God, now I'm laughing hysterically at my own brilliance. This will show Lila Fowler what I think about her and all her filthy money! I can't wait to bring her the script.

Chapter
Nine

Sam sat at the breakfast table, crunching away at a heaping bowl of Cap'n Crunch, when Elizabeth came down and poured herself a cup of coffee. *Gulp.* Sam had been hoping to avoid Elizabeth today since he still hadn't given her the list of questions he was supposedly working on for the nonexistent documentary about her elementary class. As soon as he saw her walk to the coffeemaker in her running clothes, he was the one who wanted to run. Or better yet, crawl under the table and hide. But he couldn't run, and he couldn't hide. It was too late. She had already seen him. More likely she had heard him loudly munching on his sugary kids' cereal from all the way upstairs.

"Morning, Elizabeth." As long as he couldn't get away, Sam figured that he should be the first to speak. That way it wouldn't look so much like he was avoiding her.

"Oh, hi, Sam. Wow, you're up early," she noted, acting impressed. "And eating breakfast too. What's up? Big day today?"

"Yeah, I've got a lot of stuff to do for school," he explained, neglecting to mention that it was the last day before filming of his movie started—the movie that Elizabeth knew nothing about.

"Gosh, you've really gotten a lot more serious about school ever since you signed up for this film class," Elizabeth marveled. "Have you done any more work on your questions for my class?"

"Um, yeah . . ." Sam hesitated. "I wrote some questions the other day, but then I had a bunch more new ideas. So I think I need to go over them again and make some revisions."

"Oh, great," Elizabeth answered. "Well, if you ever want me to look at them, just let me know. And, um, Sam?"

"Yeah, what is it?"

"Well, I sort of wrote up some questions too," Elizabeth began, seeming slightly nervous about bringing it up. "And I know it's your movie and everything, and I don't want to be horning in on your project, but I thought they might be good, at least as thought starters, even if you don't want to use them."

"Oh, that's great!" Sam answered enthusiastically. For a second he thought Elizabeth was going to pressure him about starting the filming. "Do you have them with you? I'd love to take a look at them."

"Great!" Elizabeth flashed a big smile, the kind that always made Sam's insides start to melt a little, even though he kept telling himself that he was no longer interested in her. "They're up in my room. Do you want me to go get them for you?"

"You don't have to do that right now," Sam answered casually. "I mean, you can if you want, but I'm about to take off, so I probably won't be able to look at them until a little bit later."

"Oh, okay." Elizabeth brought her cup of coffee over to the table and sat down across from Sam. "Well, I'll just leave them in your room for you, and you can take a look at them whenever you get a chance."

"Cool." Sam looked up from his cereal and smiled. He was happy to have Elizabeth's questions as another stalling device to delay getting started on the documentary, which he was still afraid might *never* get started. "I'll take a look at them when I get back tonight."

"Super!" Elizabeth flashed another big smile, but this time a feeling of guilt crept through Sam's body at her excitement over a project that he was afraid might never come to fruition. He knew that sooner or later he'd have to tell her about the other movies he had to do for his class. But lately things had been going so well between them that he didn't want to ruin it.

Sam took the last bite of cereal and slurped down the milk out of the bottom of the bowl. "Well, I better get going, Elizabeth. I've got to do a couple of errands on my way to school. Have a nice run, okay?"

"All right, and I'll leave those questions for you in your room."

"Cool, I'll take a look at them and tell you what I think." Sam got up from the table and made a point of washing out his cereal bowl in the sink and leaving it in the dish drainer. He left the room, feeling a combination of self-satisfaction and extreme guilt.

Sam grabbed his finished script out of his room and rushed over to the SVU campus, eager to deliver it to Lila. He was a little nervous about her reading it since it was such an obvious parody of her. He wondered if she might get upset, which was what deep down he really wanted. He also had to admit that he was a little nervous, ascending the steps to Theta house. He had never been to a sorority house before and somehow pictured a bunch of cute coeds running around in their underwear. But since he had called before coming over, he figured Lila would have gotten the girls on their best behavior. On second thought, knowing Lila, she might have planned an entire striptease for Sam's benefit just to mess with him.

Sam walked up the long walkway and marveled at the lush green lawn on either side of him. There was absolutely nothing like this on the OCC campus. They barely had any lawns at all, not to mention big houses full of rich girls. He used the big brass knocker to rap against the looming, dark wooden door before him. He had to wait a couple of minutes before the door swung open. And when it did, there was Lila. Once again she looked incredible.

"Hi, Sammy!" she sang, leaning forward to peck him on the cheek. She waved her hand for him to come inside, and as he did, she did a pirouette, no doubt to show off the backless part of her pink batik shirt, which she wore with black capris and platform sandals. She looked like she was dressed for a party, but Sam knew from their phone conversation that she was really on her way to history class.

"Hi, Lila." Sam thrust the script toward her. "I know you have to get to class, so I'll just give you this and go."

"Oh, I have a few minutes, Sam," she said, leading him toward the big staircase. "Come up to my room with me while I get my stuff. Besides, I want to take a look at this script. You know I've been dying to read it."

Sam proceeded with caution, wondering what sick surprise Lila might have waiting for him at the top of the stairs. When they reached her room on the second floor, Sam was dumbstruck. It was like a palace. For one thing, the room was five times bigger than Sam's bedroom at the house. And it had polished wood floors, with a huge oriental rug in the middle of the room. Gustav Klimt prints hung on her walls in gilded frames. At least Sam thought they were prints. But he wouldn't have been too surprised if she told him they were originals. He marveled at her media center, complete with fifty-inch TV and a stereo that probably cost twice as much as Sam's car. An Apple G4 sat on an antique rolltop desk, and Sam noticed a walk-in closet overflowing with clothes. The focal point of the room was a huge canopy bed, covered with pillows resting on a fluffy white comforter.

"Welcome to my humble abode," Lila announced, making a sweeping gesture like one of the showcase models on *The Price Is Right*.

All Sam could say was, "Whoa."

Lila started poring over the script, and she hadn't even turned the page before she started giggling. Sam watched, enraptured, as she read his work. Her eyes sparkled as her giggles evolved into genuine laughter, her head nodding approval throughout the reading.

By the time she reached page three, she was laughing hysterically, and it was definitely *with* the script, not *at* it. Sam couldn't believe it: She was obviously delighted with the whole thing.

"Oh, Sam!" she exclaimed, after she had read it straight through without letting her eyes wander once. "This is so great! It's adorable. It's so *funny*. Like you wrote it especially for me."

"Really?" Sam asked incredulously.

"Really, Sam," Lila answered, looking him in the eye. "I never thought I'd hear myself telling you this, but you're very talented."

"You mean, you're not pissed off or anything about the character?" Sam asked tentatively.

"Why?" Lila asked. "Because it's all about me?"

"Well . . . yeah."

"No, Sam. I think it's a total scream." Lila looked over the first page again before returning her eyes to Sam. "I'm serious—I think this is really good."

"And you're not angry." Sam tried again to confirm.

"Do I look like I'm angry? I love it," she gushed. "Sam, don't you think I know how to laugh at myself? I know I'm rich. I know I always get what I want."

The butterflies in Sam's stomach returned. Suddenly he was exhilarated to be alone with Lila in her palatial bedroom. Especially now that she thought he was a genius. And now that he knew she possessed a degree of self-awareness and humor about herself that he had never realized was there. Finally he was willing to admit to himself how hopelessly attracted to her he really was.

"You *always* get what you want?" Sam asked suggestively.

"Yup." Lila looked Sam directly in the eye and almost imperceptibly ran the tip of her tongue across the bottom of her upper lip.

Sam slightly lowered his head and gazed up at her, his eyebrows cocked. "So, what do you want right now, Lila?"

Lila pursed her lips, as if she had to think about it for a moment, and languorously looked Sam down and up, from head to toe and back up again.

She was about to answer when a sharp rapping on her open door called their attention to the doorway. A bleach-blond Theta sister stuck her head in the room. "Lila, let's go; we're going to be late for class—oops! I didn't know you had company."

The girl popped her head back out of the doorway and disappeared down the hall, calling out, "Sorry, Lila!"

Lila returned her attention to Sam, but the pregnant moment of seconds before was already deflated. "I guess we'll have to finish this little conversation some other time." And then she called to her friend in the hallway, "Kerri! Wait for me downstairs. I'll be right there."

Lila walked out of the room, and Sam followed, shaking his head in disbelief. *Well, well, well,* he thought. *That was one major flirting episode. Very, very interesting.*

Sam and Chris were standing at the edge of the OCC campus, rehearsing lines for Chris's movie. Sam wasn't all that impressed with her script except for one thing: She had cast him to play the love interest opposite her in her lockout story. The film was about a young college student who locked herself out of her dorm room and then fell in love with the maintenance man who was called to let her back in. Sam liked the idea of playing an OCC maintenance man, mainly because he got to wear one of their powder blue jumpsuits with the silver piping that he had always admired. But he was also taken with the idea of being Chris's on-screen love interest. And since she was the one who had cast him, he had to believe that she was interested in real life too.

So suddenly things were going pretty well for Sam in the ladies department. Elizabeth was being extra nice to him, Lila had nearly seduced him in her room that morning (and at the very least, she thought he was a cinematic genius), and now Chris was relying on him for his technical expertise, as well as his acting talent, and hopefully the on-screen chemistry that would spark between the two of them. If only the script wasn't so dumb!

And Sam would have liked a little more direction from the director too.

"Are you sure this is how you want this scene to go?" Sam asked her. "I mean, would this maintenance guy really try to kiss her right here in the middle of campus, after they just met five minutes ago? Couldn't he, like, lose his job?"

"Oh." Chris looked surprised. "Maybe you're right. But the film is only four minutes long, so they have to kiss pretty soon—if not in this scene, then probably in the next one."

"Well, do they have to kiss at all?" Sam asked. "I mean, don't get me wrong. I'm all for filming a make-out scene with you. I'm just not sure that it makes the most sense for these characters in this particular story line."

"Maybe you're right," Chris conceded. "How do you think the scene should go?"

"Chris, why do you keep doing that?" Sam asked impatiently.

"Doing what?" she asked cluelessly.

"Deferring to me every time I make a comment or ask you a question about a scene," Sam clarified. "I mean, it's your movie. Don't you want to do it your way or at least tell me why you wrote it the way you did instead of just accepting everything I say that might be wrong with it?"

"Yeah, I guess you're right," Chris said timidly.

"There you go again!" Sam shouted, exacerbated.

Suddenly he was distracted by a honking car horn. Sam turned around to see Lila pulling up to the curb in her black Porsche. She got out of the car and motioned for Sam to go over to her. He looked at Chris, as if to ask his director's permission to be excused from rehearsal, and she answered with a dirty look.

"I'll be right back," Sam told Chris. "But just think about what I said—about the kiss, I mean."

Sam walked over to where Lila was leaning against her car. "What are you doing here? We don't start filming until tomorrow, remember?"

Lila rolled her sparkling brown eyes and handed Sam a manila envelope. "I know, Sam. I just saw you this morning, remember? I just wanted to give you this."

"Huh? What is it?" Sam wondered, looking down at the envelope in his hands.

"It's your script," Lila explained. "I made a few changes."

"What?" Sam couldn't believe what he was hearing, even coming from Lila. "*You* made *changes* to *my* script?"

"Yeah, don't have a hippopotamus, Sam." Lila put her hands on her hips. "Your script is great; don't get me wrong. I told you: I loved it. It's just that I thought it could use a little work, especially if I'm going to be starring in it. Once you look it over, I'm sure you'll agree with me that it's better this way."

"How dare you make changes to my script!" Sam yelled, suddenly aware that he was making a scene, having a screaming fight with a gorgeous girl next to an expensive sports car.

"I only did what I thought was necessary," Lila protested.

"No, I don't think so," Sam answered evenly, trying to regain his composure. "Lila, I don't think you understand. This is my project. I wrote it, I'm directing it, and you are merely an actor. Understand?"

"I understand that you're full of it," Lila responded calmly. "I understand that you've been taking some stupid film class for exactly one week and now you think you're James Cameron or something."

"Oh, please," Sam answered. He would have liked to come back with something more biting than that, but her James Cameron comment hit a little too close to home.

"*Oh, please,* yourself," Lila snapped back. "Why don't you go back to your mousy little girlfriend over there who never has a thing to say about anything? Don't think I don't know why you're with her, Sam. You obviously only date dumb blond bimbos because you can't accept being challenged by a woman, especially a woman who's superior to you."

"Oh, you're superior to me?" Sam huffed. "Just because you're rich and you get whatever you want handed to you on a silver platter? And why don't you leave Chris out of this? She's not dumb, and she's not a bimbo. She's just a little quiet. And furthermore, why don't you mind your own business!"

"Oh, this is my business, Sam," Lila answered icily. "For one thing, I'm the star of this movie. And for another, since I paid for that lens you're using, the one that's going to make me look so divine on the big screen. So you owe me big time for getting you the proper equipment and for lending my beauty and talent to your movie."

"Why do you insist on thinking you're the star of some kind of important movie, Lila? This is hardly a 'movie' at all. What it is is a four-minute student project, so why don't you just get over yourself?"

"Whatever, Sam," Lila answered with a shrug. "All I can say is that I suggest you take a look at my script changes and we can talk on set tomorrow."

And with that Lila walked around to the other

side of the car, slid into the driver's seat, and sped away. Sam was left holding the envelope.

THOUGHT-BOOK ENTRY

So, it looks like Lila Fowler is one serious freak of nature. I can't seem to figure her out. She's all over the map. Telling me I'm a genius one moment and then changing my script the next. First she's totally flirting with me, and then she's going ballistic and dissing me because she thinks I think I'm some kind of big-shot director or something. It's not that I think I'm something I'm not—I just don't appreciate her trying to take over my movie. I mean, it was bad enough that she forced her way into it in the first place by buying that lens, but now she thinks she can rewrite my script? I haven't even been able to look at her changes yet. The whole thing just pisses me off too much.

And here I was, thinking I might be able to get busy with her off set! What's the deal with her anyway? One minute she acts one way, and then the next minute she's acting totally the opposite. Oh, yeah, now I get it. She's a woman. The female mind: You figure it out, Thought Book, because I sure as hell can't.

I wonder if she'll drop out of the film if I don't use her changes for the script. At this point I don't even care. She's so erratic and so hard to deal with, it might be a blessing in disguise. The only problem is, we start shooting tomorrow!

And what was the deal with her bad mouthing Chris like that?! What did Chris ever do to her? Maybe she's just jealous. Yeah, right! Like Lila Fowler has even thought twice about me except as a vehicle to put her in some dumb student film, which I don't even know why she wants to be in in the first place. Man, she bugs me so much! So why can't I get her out of my mind? Chris is the one I should really be going after. Sweet, easygoing, quiet, beer-loving Chris Childress. So how come every time I try to picture me and Chris together, Lila rears her evil head inside my mind?

Chapter
Ten

"Camera," Sam called out.

"Speed," Miguel reported.

"Sound," Leslie murmured quietly.

"And . . . *action*," Sam said intently.

For the eleventh time Lila emptied her black leather handbag on the marble bench outside Theta house. Wallet, lipstick, tissues, cell phone, pencils, French-franc coins, PalmPilot, Teeny Beanie Babies swan, compact, piece after piece materialized for the camera and failed to be house keys. The ingenue (Lila) sighed nervously at the locked door and windows of the antique mansion. The corners of her eyes narrowed ever so slightly in concern, and she touched a manicured hand to a loose brunette curl.

"And . . . cut!" Sam exhorted. "All right! I think we got it! Lila, that was great. Team, let's set up for shot six!"

The crew turned to their respective pieces of equipment to break them down to transport them to Nairopa Avenue, the boutique district near SVU, where they were going to shoot the shopping scenes. Lila had learned (Sam didn't know how) that Mike drove a pickup truck, and not only was she able to commandeer use of the vehicle, but she was able to coerce the scraggly pug into taking over keeping track of all the tech details for the mobile shoot. Her kitten-with-a-whip routine had transformed snarling Mike and sullen Leslie into willing lapdogs. Miguel operated as unofficial go-between for her and Chris, who had retreated behind the oversized hood of her black sweatshirt and black sunglasses and lurked silently among the lights like a chastened Darth Vader.

Sam smiled broadly as they stepped casually to Lila's Porsche, parked illegally at the curb. Lila had convinced him that the police never ticket at a movie shoot, and it appeared that she might be right. At this point Sam felt willing to believe just about anything she might say. First, that morning he had read her script changes, and within a couple of minutes he had realized that they were for the most part pretty good. A lot of it was just the addition of detail, things that she could have just done on her own once they started shooting, like the parade of accessories that had appeared from her handbag. She had carefully selected each one and even decided in advance what order they would come out and where she would place them. She had added a couple of lines for herself, but Sam didn't mind that either. She had a lot of practice talking to people about buying things from them.

This is going to be so good, Sam contemplated happily. After the ongoing debacle with Elizabeth's school and seeing firsthand how difficult simple-seeming things could turn out to be, he had begun to appreciate the value of keeping things simple. *Complications don't add together,* he calculated, *they multiply.* The best part about working with Lila had turned out to be that she was all business—just the opposite of what he would have expected. Sam had thought she would be whiny and easily distracted. On the contrary: She had memorized her lines, including of course her new ones, and the precisely planned blocking out of the scenes, and from the moment she appeared on the set in a loose cotton blouse and men's striped trousers, she had simply, ruthlessly, and effectively focused everyone's attention on the matter at hand: making a decent first student film, putting her face on the screen, and keeping out of her way as she confabulated with her director.

Lila whipped her sports car left as the traffic light slipped from yellow to red. The truck was stuck behind them at the light, and Sam turned back to look. Mike, behind the wheel, was screaming at Miguel, who rode in the middle of the cab with a clipboard on his knees, and Leslie, who had pressed his cheek to the passenger-side window and appeared to be asleep. Chris rode in the back of the pickup, looking for all the world like a black Labrador retriever in her huge black sweatshirt flapping in the breeze.

"Whoops," said Sam.

"I know," Lila said. "We'll catch up with them at the next site. I wanted to take a little detour."

Sam's heart raced. What was she thinking? "Uh, Lila," he blurted out, "shouldn't we keep our minds on the shoot?"

"Uh-huh," she purred, making another rapid left turn with tires squealing. Sam looked around nervously to see if there were any cop cars around. He wanted to ask her to drive a little slower, but he didn't want to seem afraid, so instead he just clung to the leather armrests. "Where are you taking us?" he demanded.

"You'll see." She smiled, shifting down to stop at a light. Her leather-gloved hand thrummed boringly on the polished mahogany stick shift. "I'm afraid some things just won't wait." Tugging a thick, stray lock back from her sunglasses, she gunned the motor like a motorcycle's.

Sam contemplated the storefronts along the avenue. "You'd better know what you're doing," he said. "I wouldn't want anything to get in the way of what we're trying to get done."

"Don't worry," she said. "As soon as I get this one thing I want, we'll be back on the blocks and shooting."

"Yeah, well, I just think we ought to stay focused, you know?" he asked uncertainly. The light turned green, and Lila swung a quick left in front of oncoming traffic. Sam shielded his eyes reflexively. But the Porsche was so quick and powerful that they were clear in a split second.

"Now," Lila said, "won't be long now." With a seemingly mad turn of the wheel she shot the car forward between a truck and the curb and pulled up outside the squawk box at a McDonald's. A tinny voice emerged. "Hello, McDonald's, take your order."

"Small fries," Lila said. "You want anything, Burgess?"

Sam stared at her in disbelief. "No, thanks."

"Suit yourself."

She pulled out and hit another quick left turn in front of a speeding taxi, dripping fries one by one onto her tongue to avoid getting any on her lipstick. Sam realized that they were on the same street they had been on when she had turned off.

Looking ahead after a couple of blocks, he wasn't surprised to see Mike's truck in front of them. Chris clung to the back of the truck, keeping her other arm on the camera. Lila slowed down to avoid overtaking them before she finished her fries.

"I don't want them to feel left out," she said, crumpling up the wrapper and tucking it under the armrest.

"Ha," Sam said.

"I don't!" she said, checking her teeth in the mirror and rubbing them with a gloved finger.

"They'll be able to smell it on your breath, Lila," he said.

"Oh, that's all right," she cooed. "You can't tell smells on film."

True enough, Sam thought. *Ever the professional.*

Sam clasped his hands with joy. "Cut!" he called out. "And wrap. That's a keeper. Thanks, guys." The crew broke into a relieved murmur. Amazingly, they had managed to work through two days' shooting in one. Sam felt immensely relieved and satisfied. Looking out from the rooftop of the parking garage where they had filmed the final scene, he contemplated the day's work well done. He felt that directing was something he could really do. It was much harder than he had anticipated: It seemed there was always a new problem, arranging the camera or making sure everything was well lit. At least he hadn't really had to worry about personnel problems: With Lila's hot-ice demeanor, combined with his own willingness to make decisions and keep the endeavor going forward, they had managed to bring their efforts together as a team pretty well for the most part, and Sam had been able to concentrate on posing and framing his pretty and enthusiastic leading lady.

The sun began to redden in the west. The crew loaded the last of the equipment into the truck, and Mike started the engine. Miguel had joined Chris in the back with the equipment, and Leslie had already taken the opportunity to go to sleep in the passenger seat. Lila had taken off without saying where she was going, but Sam noticed that she was sitting in her car, talking into her cell phone. He sighed and turned back to watch the sunset.

He sure had misjudged Lila Fowler, he said to himself for the umpteenth time that day. He had really lucked out getting picked by her as a target for her will and credit card. He was confident that the film was going to be the best in the class—how could it not? He took his sunglasses out of his shirt pocket and wrapped them over his eyes to be able to enjoy the sunset directly. After a little while he heard Lila's car door close and the clicking of her heels as she came over to join him by the low wall.

"Well, Mr. Director," she said. "It seems we make quite a team." She sat down and crossed her legs in her suit pants. One black high-heeled sandal dangled from a toe.

Sam smiled generously. "Well, Ms. Starlet," he allowed, "I just have to thank you again for your professionalism and talent."

"Oh, you should thank yourself for bringing it out in me," she responded, turning from the setting sun to face him. The streaming red rays danced in the polished gold of her sunglasses. Sam cocked his head at her lazily. After spending the entire afternoon talking comfortably and earnestly about what she was going to do with every inch of her body and mind, he no longer felt like they were completely different people. He smiled at her again. "So, you're not always this focused?"

She paused slightly, allowing her lips to part, and raised her hand to pull her long, curly chestnut hair forward and around her neck. "I guess it's all a matter of inspiration," she cooed softly.

Sam leaned closer to her, smoothly, gently bringing his lips down to meet hers. He had been wanting to do it for hours, and now he was going to. The moment was perfect, and they had been so close all day. . . . He pressed his lips slowly but firmly against hers, which were warm and soft.

Lila kissed him back, really kissed him. She

caught his face in her hands and held him for a long, sweet one. He felt like he no longer had to think but just to *do*. He put his arm around her shoulders and drew her closer.

After their kisses began to subside, Lila rested her cheek against his shirt and shuddered slightly against his chest. "Well," Sam said. "Who'd have thought?"

"I'd have thought," she replied. He could feel her breathing against him. He put his finger under her jaw to gently raise her lips to kiss them again. The last of the sun's rays shot wildly through the glass-and-steel canyons of the city.

"Lila," he said. "Why'd you do all this? I mean, the movie and all. You and I both know it's just a dorky intro-to-film exercise. You could at least have gotten in one of the films the seniors are making. At least they know how to work the equipment. This is pretty much the bottom of the barrel."

"I thought it would be *fun*," she said, believably enough. "If I'm going to have to work with OCC students, I don't want to have to work with the ones who want to make a lifetime out of it. Do you think I wanted to argue with some OCC spud-tech dork? No, thanks. No, I was perfectly satisfied with the Mikes and the other ones. At least they know how to do what they're told." Sam winced at her choice of words. He half expected her to complain how hard it was to get good help these days.

"Besides, you're cute and funny," she said, and put her finger on the side of his nose. "And you were going to make a movie, and, well, maybe to make Bruce jealous."

"Bruce?" Sam asked. "Bruce *who?*"

Lila appeared puzzled. "Bruce who what?" she repeated.

"Who's Bruce?"

"Bruce Patman! Who'd you think?"

"Who the hell is Bruce Patman?" Sam exclaimed.

"Bruce *Patman,*" Lila said. "You *know* him. He's my *boyfriend,* Sam."

"I do not!" Sam shot back. "I've never heard of the guy in my life!"

"Because he's on a semester-abroad program," Lila explained, a little pout forming on the lips he just kissed—foolishly kissed. "He won't be back until Christmas or New Year's."

Sam cringed inside. He vaguely recalled those details attending one or another of the SVU crew who showed up at the twins' functions. Lila had a boyfriend? *Duh,* he thought. *I shoulda known.* "Oh," he said, his narrowed eyes hidden behind his sunglasses. He couldn't see her eyes either. "Oh, yeah, Bruce. I think I heard Jess mention him a few times."

Lila leaned in for another kiss, her head tilting to the side in anticipation mixed with apprehension.

188

Sam could tell that she was glad to have that worked out. He shifted back slightly, drinking in the vision of this daring and carefree beauty who thought she could have anything she wanted and had thrown the full weight of her charms and powers behind getting him. And for what? Just to sneak around behind her boyfriend's back? Sam felt used. For a moment anger flashed through him in a fiery streak, and then he grew somber. It was starting to get chilly.

"Lila," Sam reproved her. "I didn't know you had a boyfriend. Why didn't you say something?"

Lila tossed her hair. "Sam," she said, "he's in *another country*. All *semester*. Anyway, flirting and making out isn't cheating cheating. I'm sure Bruce is seeing girls in Paris. And besides, what's so wrong with having a little harmless fun with someone of the opposite sex?"

"How romantic," he uttered tonelessly. She sounded like most of the guy jerks he knew!

Lila pursed her lips slightly in impatience. "Sam?" she said, calling him up short, "take it easy, huh? It's nice up here, but it's nicer at Gargamel's at around seven-thirty, which is when we have dinner reservations."

Sam stared at her evenly. He wanted to go home. "I don't think so," he answered.

Lila gave him a glance that said she appreciated his effort, but she didn't feel like playing this game right now. "Sam," she said. "I thought you were such a big-time player. I had no idea you actually had some morals. Maybe we're not cut from the same cloth, as they say, after all."

Sam felt hurt and confused. *I am a big-time player,* he thought. *So what's wrong with me?*

"Yeah," he said, "well, don't give up quite yet. But I don't think I'm ready to go any farther on a first date."

Lila smiled and gave his hand a squeeze.

Why did Sam feel so bad? What was going on here?

THOUGHT-BOOK ENTRY

Well, quite a day today. You'll never guess who I hooked up with. The richest, snobbiest girl at SVU and me making out after the film shoot. Am I crazy? I can't describe the effect she was having on me. The kissing was incredible. The whole day was incredible. Turns out Lila has a lot more going for her than I ever would have thought. She's not just beautiful; she also knows what she wants and she knows how to get it. And today she and I wanted pretty much the same thing. And that was pretty incredible.

Yeah, Lila is full of surprises. Like a boyfriend.

Whoops. I guess I should have known. But Thought Book, I didn't. I guess that's too bad. I hope she doesn't tell him.

Or maybe it's not such a bad thing. Lila and I

would never be any good together. Or would we? No way. Question: Would she have gone for me like she did if she didn't have a boyfriend? Answer: No way. Not like she did. But there was something there. I didn't imagine that. She would have gone for me—if she had ended up being in my movie, which she probably would never have done if Frenchy was home to take care of business.

Which is kind of too bad. Dude, I know I want to work with her again. That chick was made for the camera.

I don't think I could ever get serious about her, though.

But who knows?

And anyway, I thought I was kind of seeing someone. I mean, Chris and I haven't made out yet, but I know I wanted to. And now I've already kissed Lila, and she was ready to throw tonight to the winds and see where we ended up. Man, am I glad I didn't go along for that. I could never see Chris after all this if I ended up sleeping with Lila. It would be weird enough as it stands just because I kissed her.

I would never be able to get it out of my mind. It would ruin the whole thing. And Lila would definitely be a short-term thing. At most.

What am I thinking? She has a boyfriend.

Yeah. In France.

*   *   *

Tuesday. Middle of the night. 4 A.M., to be precise, thank you very much.

I can't sleep. This sucks. This is crazy. If there's one thing I can always do, it's fall asleep.

It's her. No, not Chris, sweet, pretty Chris. It's the other one. The dark mistress.

Lila. I cannot get Lila Fowler out of my mind.

This is stupid. She's everything I'm not. She likes to flash around Daddy's cash. She goes shopping five days a week. She's pledge mistress at her sorority—please!

So why am I so hung up on her?

Opposites attract, Sam-o.

No, Sam-o, Lila and I are not opposites. We're different species altogether.

I have got to get to sleep. I am not going to be able to get to sleep.

The worst part is that all the things that used to drive me crazy about her still drive me crazy but now in a different way. Her arrogance: I hated that. Now it turns me on. I am losing it. It all has me going.

Those stupid manicured fingernails used to remind me of the way Mrs. Farmer polished her poodle's toenails when I was a kid. Now I can't stop seeing them.

It feels different somehow. It feels funny. I can't describe it. I want hot chocolate.

What kind of wuss am I turning into?

I can't say I never tried to stop her from thinking

that I had more women than I knew what to do with. This is what I always thought I wanted. Mr. Big-Time Player. The Mack. Whatever: Why am I all messed up now that she's turned the tables on me?

I have no idea what I'm in for.

Chapter
Eleven

Sam was feeling awfully good today. It was the last day of filming on the SVU campus, and everything was running smoothly. Or at least, as smoothly as could be expected after the beauty turned ugliness that happened at the end of the shoot the day before. Lila was still acting like a prima donna and getting uptight whenever Sam said as much as two words to Chris. But she still knew all her lines, her acting was phenomenal, and she looked great as always. Now that Sam knew about Bruce, though, he was trying to look at her only when necessary, and he was trying to keep everything on the up-and-up. Purely professional the whole way. But still, Bruce or no Bruce, Sam couldn't deny the feelings he had for Lila, especially after that kiss last night.

But after working so closely with Chris these past few days, he wasn't ready to deny his feelings for her either, and he was still enjoying the closeness. Chris was working today as DP, director of photography, so they had plenty of chances to consult with each other about camera angles, lighting, and basically everything else that had anything to do with the movie. In between shots Sam kept checking footage, and he was relying more and more on Chris's judgment when it came to lighting choices and other minutiae. Even though she wasn't the smartest person on set and it took her a while to get the hang of a lot of the equipment, Sam had to admit that Chris had a good eye and a pretty good knack for what looked and sounded right on film.

"Chris, could you come here for a second? I want to get your opinion on something," Sam called to her where she was standing behind the camera.

Chris came over to where Sam was viewing some of the footage on a tiny monitor. She had to get close to him, crouching with her shoulder butting up against Sam's chest, so they could both watch at the same time.

"Right there, did you hear that?" Sam asked, referring to what he thought was a barely audible buzzing. He couldn't figure out where it was coming from. "What is that noise? Was that in the other takes?"

"What?" Chris asked. "What are you talking about?"

"I don't know; it's like a buzzing or something," Sam tried to explain. "I can't figure out where it's coming from."

"Roll it back and let me listen for it again," Chris said, leaning closer to the monitor and to Sam.

"Excuse me, Sam," Lila butted in, coming over to the monitor from her place on the set. "But last time I checked, wasn't Chris the DP?"

"Yeah, why?" Sam asked, puzzled and slightly perturbed.

"Well, I was just wondering why you're asking her questions about sound when Mike is doing sound and Chris is supposed to be in charge of cameras and lighting," Lila said knowingly.

"That's a very good point, Ms. Fowler," Sam answered sarcastically. "But last time I checked, you were the actress in this scene and not the assistant director. So if you wouldn't mind, could you please return to your place on set? I'll get back to your scene in a moment."

"Fine," Lila huffed, and stomped back over to her spot in front of the camera.

When they rolled the footage again, Chris

watched and listened intently but merely shrugged when it was over. "I don't know, Sam; I don't hear anything."

"See, Sam?" Lila said from across the set. "I told you she didn't know anything."

Sam noticed Chris rolling her eyes, and he was grateful she didn't say anything back to Lila. It would have only made things worse.

"Okay, everyone," Sam called out. "Places."

Everyone returned to their respective duties, but before Sam could call for action, Chris called him over. "Sam, this lever is, like, stuck or something."

Sam walked quickly over to Chris. Time was of the essence now since the natural lighting was perfect and the sun wouldn't stick around forever. "What is it?"

"It's this, right here. I'm trying to adjust the camera height," she explained, "but I can't quite seem to release this."

"Here, let me try," Sam offered, leaning over her shoulder so that their cheeks were practically touching. Sam was so close to Chris that with each breath, he inhaled a mixture of her subtle perfume and the scent of her shampoo—lilacs mingling with lavender. It smelled delicious, and Sam had a hard time concealing his delight. A serene smile crossed his face as he breathed deeply, at the same time trying to figure out how to release the lever.

"Oh, please!" Lila called from in front of the camera. "Why don't you two just get a room already!"

Chris let out a loud, exasperated sigh. Apparently she had heard enough of Lila's snide remarks. In uncharacteristic fashion she looked up at Lila and, shaking her head with an ugly scowl on her face, said, "You know, Lila, if you were a better actress, you might have an easier time concealing your jealousy!"

Lila tilted her head and matched Chris scowl for scowl. "Well, Chris, if you were a competent director of photography, we would have already finished filming this scene, and I'd be talking on my cell phone to my boyfriend right now. That way you wouldn't have to confuse my impatience at your total lack of professionalism with something as trite and laughable as jealousy."

"Professionalism?" Chris scoffed. "In case you're somehow lost in your movie-star fantasy, let me just remind you that this is a *student film*, Lila. There's no place for professionalism here because we're not professionals. Just like you, none of us has ever done this before."

"Never done this before?" Lila huffed. "Are you saying I've never acted before?"

"Not unless you count acting like a spoiled brat!" Chris fired back.

Touché! Sam thought. *And déjà vu!*

But he didn't have time right now for any cat-fights between cast and crew. "Ladies!" he shouted. "Can we please have quiet on the set so we can just get through this scene? Please!"

Just as he was shouting his second "please," Sam looked up and noticed Elizabeth walking by the set.

Uh-oh.

If the commotion of the shoot hadn't already drawn her attention, his little outburst most certainly had. Elizabeth caught his eye, and he registered on her face an expression of confusion, quickly followed by revelation. He was afraid that the movie he'd been concealing from her all along was suddenly out in the open.

Sam ran over to Elizabeth, who was staring at the surrounding proceedings. Despite his attempted demonstration of authority, he wondered if perhaps Elizabeth still didn't realize that he was in charge of the set. That in fact this was Sam's movie. Maybe he could divert her attention before she was able to figure it out.

"Elizabeth, hey!" he greeted her with a big, dumb smile.

"Hi, Sam," she said cheerfully. "This is so

great, getting to see you working on one of your classmates' movies. I didn't know you were going to be filming at SVU. You should have told me about it, and I would have stopped by earlier. What's this one about?"

"Um, it's—um . . . ," Sam stammered.

"Oh, I can tell you're busy; you can tell me about it later," Elizabeth said. "Do you mind if I watch, though? What's your job on this one anyway?"

"It's, um, well, don't you have to get to class or something?" Sam rambled, completely flustered. "It's pretty boring to watch anyway unless you're, like, involved in it."

"Hey!" Elizabeth shouted. "Isn't that Lila? What's she doing here? Is she in this movie?"

"Oh, yeah, she's one of the extras," Sam lied. "Just kind of walked on the set, and we decided to use her."

Sam could practically see Elizabeth's brain at work as she scanned the set and looked him suspiciously up and down. "Wait a second, Sam," she finally said. "This is your movie, isn't it?"

All Sam could do was look at the ground and nod. At this point there was no use in lying.

"So this is why you've been putting me off?" she demanded, anger rising in her voice. "You're making *another* movie?"

"Yeah, well, this is a different project my professor's making me work on," Sam lamely tried to explain. "You know, before we move on to documentary."

Suddenly Sam noticed Chris walking over to him. "Documentary?" Chris asked in a puzzled voice. "What documentary?"

"You know, Chris. The documentary I've been telling you about," Sam answered, screwing up his eyes in a silent effort to get her to go along with his farce.

"There isn't any documentary project for this class," Chris insisted. "There's just the lockout piece and two other shorts. What are you talking about, Sam?"

Sam looked pleadingly at Elizabeth, whose eyes suddenly narrowed into slits.

"I am so outta here," Elizabeth spat, and turned to walk quickly away.

Sam turned to Chris. "Great! Thanks a lot, Chris."

Chris just shrugged and shook her head, looking confused and slightly irritated. And Sam didn't have time to explain what she had just done—what *he* had just done. He had to catch up with Elizabeth and explain himself.

He jogged after her. "Elizabeth, wait up! Let me explain."

"Don't bother, Sam," she called coldly over her shoulder. "I've heard enough of your stupid lies!"

Sam walked doggedly back to the set, silently kicking himself for not leveling with Elizabeth earlier about his confusion over film class. If he had only been honest with her, he could have avoided the whole mess that he was in the middle of right now.

"Okay, everyone, let's just finish this shot and it'll be a wrap," he announced, trying to regain control over the film shoot.

Chris threw down her headphones in a huff. "I don't think so, Sam."

"Wait a second, Chris." Sam shot her a puzzled look. "What don't you think? What's the matter?"

"I don't *think* I can work under these conditions anymore. I'm leaving."

"What are you talking about? What conditions?" Sam ran a frustrated hand through his hair and looked at her pleadingly.

"First of all, your little friend over there, Miss Prima Donna Actress, who can't seem to separate herself from the role she's playing, has been getting on my nerves since this movie began," Chris spewed. "And now in the middle of a shot you're running off to attend to one of your other little girlfriends, who's not even involved in the movie."

"Hey, take it easy, Chris," Sam said in his most soothing voice. "I know it's been a long day, but can't you just stick around for this last shot? We really need you."

Chris just stood there, staring coldly at Sam and shaking her head.

What happened to nice, easygoing Chris? he wondered. *Since when did all the women in my life decide to turn against me?*

Lila spoke up from across the set. "Now look who's suffering from pangs of jealousy, *Chris*."

"You shut up!" Chris shouted back.

"Lila, please," Sam begged. "Both of you, can't we just finish this shot and go home?"

Chris let out another long sigh and put her headphones back on. "Okay, let's go, then. And then I'm leaving."

Sam looked around at the guys on the set, who were all suddenly silent, looking at the ground and shaking their heads. Like they were embarrassed to even be associated with the proceedings. "So, are you all ready? Can we roll this? Lila?"

Lila huffed herself into position, and Sam called for action. Miraculously the scene came off without a hitch. Everyone on set silently hurried to pack up their equipment. Chris left without saying another word.

Mike, Miguel, and Leslie stood around, waiting for Sam to say something, but all he could think of was, "Thanks, guys. I guess I'll see you in class Wednesday."

They all nodded solemnly, and they too left without saying anything. The only person left on the set with Sam was Lila. Sam shook his head in disbelief. He should have been feeling on top of the world. His first shoot was in the can, ready for editing. This was huge. But Sam was stuck with a sour taste in his mouth. He had somehow blown it with Chris without even knowing what was happening. She was obviously pissed, and he'd be lucky if she ever spoke to him again, let alone still wanted him in her movie.

And once again he had ruined his tenuous friendship with Elizabeth. He had the feeling she was back to hating him now, just like at the end of their summer fling. So the only woman left was Lila, and she had some complicated thing going on with her absentee boyfriend, Bruce.

Sam wondered if he could salvage the fleeting chemistry they had shared. He wanted to ask her out, but of course he was totally broke. He looked up to see her standing expectantly a few feet away. "Hey, Lila, I'm sorry the shoot had to end the way it did, with all the added drama and everything. But I just wanted to let you know, I think you did really great. Thanks for being in my movie."

Lila smiled a genuine smile. "You were great too, Sam. None of this could have come off as well as it did without your great script. And you're a pretty decent director too. At least when there isn't too much fur flying on the set."

Maybe there was hope for him and Lila after all, Sam thought. "So, do you want to maybe get together sometime, Lila?" he asked, mustering all his confidence. "I could make you a nice home-cooked meal over at the house."

"Thanks, Sam," Lila said coolly. "But I don't do home cooked."

"Oh. Yeah. Right. It figures," Sam said glumly.

Lila's voice brightened. "Thanks for asking, though, Sam. You're a sweet guy. You really are. But I just think it would be too weird coming to your house for dinner, especially with Jessica living there and everything."

"Yeah, I guess you're right." Sam was about to propose some kind of alternative, but Lila wasn't finished talking.

"Besides, I talked to Bruce this morning," she went on, "and I think everything is going to work out after all. He's not actually seeing anyone, and he doesn't want me to either. So I guess I'm not really available anymore."

"So that kiss last night really didn't mean anything," Sam surmised.

"No, it did, Sam," Lila insisted. "You're cute and sweet, and I really do like you, but come on, it would never work. Even if Bruce was out of the picture, just think about it. You and me? We'd wind up killing each other."

When Sam thought about it, he had to admit that she was right. "Yeah, I guess you have a point there, Lila."

"But hey. Look on the bright side," Lila added hopefully. "We made a great movie together, didn't we?"

"Yeah, I guess we did," Sam agreed. "I guess we did make a pretty great movie."

Chapter Twelve

Finished watching the last of the footage. No disasters. Lucky. Really, it looks pretty good overall. I don't know; I'll have to watch it again. But I have a lot of decent stuff to work with. It looks like the editing is going to be a pretty major task, though. Camera work is okay. Some focus problems. The camera loves Lila, of course.

Lila loves the camera too. Lila loves Bruce, and Bruce wuvs Wiwa too.

I think I might have lucked out there too. That could have ended up really messed up. Would have. Probably wouldn't have been worth the grief.

Like that's ever stopped me before.

Regrets are just par for the course. I would have liked to have been able to spend a little more time with Lila and then not gotten involved with her

209

when I found out she had a boyfriend. I probably wouldn't feel any worse right now.

I wonder how mad Chris is going to stay. For the whole rest of the semester we have to work together. I guess I think she'll probably get over it. I don't know. It's not like I really get her. She seems to have something together under there, but she sure is squirrelly. So totally opposite to Lila. I guess I can't really say I chose Lila either—she chose me. I guess she really had everything taken care of from the beginning. Little did Chris know she was in the path of a ship. Small crafts get swamped.

I wonder if either of them will try to make more movies. Not with me if they can help it, I'm guessing. Lila ought to get herself an agent. I bet Chris'll end up making something worth watching before it's over. Not that maintenance-man thing, though. That was weird.

And Elizabeth. Wow. I really thought I might be able to impress her. That was pretty stupid. And now it's all screwed up with her, that's for sure. Mr. Filmmaker. What a joke. Sad Sam is more like it.

She'll hold it like a grudge. This one's going to be an endurance match.

I do it for the art; that's got to be it. That's where it's all at. It all comes back to the art. Otherwise it's still just college.

I still want to make the documentary. That's

something worth doing. Not just for Elizabeth, though, or for the kids, but for me too. If I have to make four-minute testaments to torture in order to get the chance to do it, then so be it.

Sam sat up straight on the edge of the couch, a Chicago White Sox hat pulled down low on his head, a backpack and a nylon windbreaker on the floor at his feet. He really had to get going, but the sight of his video game in the corner caught his eye, and he had been playing just one more game for the last forty minutes. He was perching on the edge of the couch and left on his hat because he was having a hard time admitting to himself how much fun it was to play after having spent the week trying to present a person on a screen for four minutes.

It looked like he wasn't going to make it to American lit. *Oh, well. There's nothing like the fresh feeling of a video game that you're really good at and haven't played in a while,* he thought joyfully. Lara Croft appeared on-screen, fighting the good fight and not giving Sam any trouble.

Neil wandered into the living room. Sam gave him a brief nod, enough not to be rude but not taking his eye off the screen for too long. It was a sort of signal he and Neil had evolved over the months they'd been housemates.

"Ah, the return of the prodigal son," Neil murmured in a welcome. "I see you've killed the fatted video game."

Sam wasn't too sure what Neil was talking about, but he had the idea Neil was making fun of him for being back to his old tar pit. "If you'd had the week I've had," he said between bursts of machine-gun fire, "you'd want to kill somebody too."

"What makes you think I don't?" Neil protested indignantly.

"Shhh," Sam said suddenly, trying to maneuver Lara out of an unlikely tight spot. He concentrated on the screen and twisted briefly in his seat.

Neil drifted off to the kitchen, and Sam heard him putting a kettle on the range top. Then his voice reappeared before him as he walked back over to Sam and plopped down beside him. "Now, how do you play this thing anyway?" he interrupted Sam's concentration nosily. Sam held the controller out of Neil's reach and tried to keep his mind on the game.

"Watch," Sam admonished him. "Hey, cut it out," he cried, fending off Neil's intrusive reach.

"Fine, then," Neil huffed pitifully. "Don't show me."

"Ah, look, you see, you don't want to die

here," Sam offered. "This is a good place not to die."

"Oh, that's helpful," Neil agreed exaggeratedly. "Don't die. Thanks. I think I get it. Lemme try." He made another move for the controller. "Which one is the button that doesn't make you die?"

"Stop," Sam complained. "It's a different one at different places in the game. See, like here, it's the left-arrow button. But sometimes it's better to go right. Dude, no!" He was talking to a looming explosion. If only he could go faster! He was so close! But he did indeed die. Or Lara did anyway. Sam paused and contemplated the living room and Neil for a moment. It was still clean in here from his having undertaken the big scrub. Somehow the place seemed empty without his half-used trash scattered around. He held the controller with his thumb on the reset button.

"So," Neil said. "How's film treatin' you?"

"Good and bad," Sam admitted. "It's a lot harder than I thought it would be."

"Yeah, I've heard it's complicated." Neil nodded sympathetically. "Even without Lila Fowler."

"So you heard about that, did you?"

"Heard about it? Sam, Jessica has been full of nothing else for a week. This place was Lila rumor

213

central. We could have published a gossip sheet. And you would have been on page one, above the fold, kid."

Sam glanced at his roomie in surprise. He should have known Lila would have been giving Jessica the daily scoop. More than daily, probably. She was probably giving Jessica a blow by blow on her constant cell-phone calls. *What else was she going to do on the phone all the time,* he thought, *check her stock prices?* He didn't care if Jessica kept track of his little adventure. At least he could count on her not spilling the beans to Elizabeth. Not that it mattered *now.* But anyway, he was reassured to recall that for some reason, Jessica usually kept dirt with Sam involved away from Elizabeth's ears. She seemed to think that the grimy details of Sam's love life weren't exactly what her sister needed to hear, a consideration that had definitely saved Sam from a few embarrassments from time to time.

Still, he thought, *I gotta remember I live in a fishbowl. As much as I try not to care what people think, I don't really need Elizabeth to hear about it if I happen to get lucky. Especially if she hears about it before I do.*

"Yeah, Sam," Neil continued, "you were hot on the *Sweet Valley Enquirer* report. Man, aren't you afraid Bruce'll get mad when he gets back?"

"Who is this Bruce guy?" Sam demanded, his interest piqued. "I forget what he looks like."

"He looks like Lila, in male form. Good-looking and beyond rich."

That actually made Sam feel better. Lila and this Bruce guy were clearly from the same place, understood their lives, understood each other. That was cool, sort of.

"I hope you don't get your butt kicked," Neil reassured him.

"Dude." Sam shook his head in reply. "The guy's a *French* major. I don't think I have a lot to worry about."

"Some of those French were tough," Neil cautioned him. "Think of Charlemagne. Napoleon. Little guy who felt he had something to prove. Guy's probably got a lot to live down, being a French major."

"Well, tell me if he comes around." Sam smirked.

Neil nodded. "You're going to get beat up *bad*," he concluded, restarting the video game and taking the controls.

Sam stood up and stretched. Talking about his leading lady had reminded him: He had to call Lila.

Neil cringed from the explosions on the screen and got up to get the kettle, which had begun to whistle. "Man, Sam, this game is way complicated," he said. "I don't see how you keep track of it."

Sam addressed his retreating back. "You get used to it, man," he said.

He ducked back into his room and dialed the phone. Lila didn't answer, so he called her on her cell. She answered breathily. "Hello?"

"Lila," Sam said. "How's it going?"

"Hi, Sam," she chattered merrily. "I was just talking about you to Gunther!"

"Gunther?" he repeated.

"Gunther says hi," Lila said.

"Who's Gunther?"

"Omigod, Sam, you don't know Gunther? Gunther Gobel? The guitar player?"

"No," Sam said, "the only Gunther I know lives with the apes in the bush."

Lila laughed. "His band, Butcher Clyde? They're releasing an album. They need someone to make a video on spec. I told him he should ask you. Sam, you'll love Butcher Clyde. They're just like you."

"We'll see," Sam demurred. "Look, Lila, the footage is great. I was thinking we should have a wrap party tonight. I mean, it's traditional."

"Okay," Lila confirmed. "If it's traditional, then party we must!"

"Great," Sam said. "I'll see you tonight, then. How about The Burgundy Room at eight?"

"Well." Lila hesitated. "The Burgundy Room kind of came and went, Sam, and I'm afraid it's pretty over."

"I've always gone there!" Sam protested. "You didn't *discover* it, Fowler."

"Okay, sexy." Lila laughed. "Anything for you."

"That's better, movie star," Sam said. "See you then."

"See ya, hottie," she repeated, and hung up.

Sam was pumped. A gray equipment case the approximate size and texture of a hard-walled suitcase standing beside his desk caught his eye. He sat down beside it on his desk chair, fingering the thickly painted letters and numbers OCC AV 22L the case bore on its heavily nicked and weathered top. He opened it up for another look.

The next unit was going to involve the use of a handheld camera, and since Sam had finished shooting his film, he had been allowed to check one out of the film department the previous afternoon. He had spent the early morning hours familiarizing himself with its controls, which were similar to the larger camera's but stripped down and compact. He liked the way the bulky, heavy instrument felt in his arms. It rested densely on his shoulder, uneager to be held motionless no matter how hard Sam tried to keep his body stiff, even standing still. When he tried to walk, the image in the eyepiece trembled and shook as if a major earthquake had hit Sweet Valley and California was falling into the sea.

Sam walked out of his room, the handheld grinding a rough edge against his neck. *This ain't video, that's for sure,* he reminded himself warily. The camera was formed mostly of steel machinery and seemed so huge and bulky that it appeared to Sam's technology-jaded eye like an unwieldy and primitive gadget from a previous era. A working antiquity. It was as if he were carrying around a big desk-model electric typewriter or a steam-powered locomotive. Still, the device had its own particular charm, and he enjoyed seeing the house through its rubber-cupped eyepiece.

Why, there was Neil, pleasantly enjoying a lovely cappuccino—well done, Neil! *And here is the trusty old staircase; better get this one on film or no one would ever know how we got to the second floor, and here's . . . Elizabeth's room! That's right, kids, this is where the magic happens. Let's see if our hostess is receiving visitors.*

Reaching out, he grasped the doorknob, trying to keep the camera balanced and in focus on his shoulder. There wasn't really enough light in the hallway for him to be able to see. Elizabeth's voice sounded through the door.

"Yeah?" she said.

"It's Sam."

"What do *you* want?" she asked.

"Show you something."

Pause. "What is it?"

Sam smiled. At least she didn't tell him to get lost. "Handheld sixteen-millimeter-film camera. Ever seen one?"

Silence.

Sam stood stolid in the hall, peering at the gloomy doorway and trying not to shift his body under the unwieldy weight. The sharp edge was starting to incise his neck. *Damn*, he thought.

"Elizabeth?"

Silence. He knocked again.

Her voice called out again. "Who is it?"

"Sam," he repeated.

"Sam, what do you want from me?"

Sam wished she would at least open the door. "Elizabeth, you ought to see this camera. It's pretty cool. If you attach it to a bike, you could make a moped." She didn't laugh.

"Look, Sam, I'm not really in the mood right now."

"Elizabeth, I'm sorry," he said naturally. "I'm sorry about the whole thing, okay? But why'd you have to be so sensitive?" He wished he hadn't said that. "I mean, look, here's the thing: I still want to make the documentary. I can't do it right away, but I need the practice anyway so I have half an idea what I'm doing when I—I mean we—get started. Okay?"

Elizabeth's voice came through the door loud and clear. He could hear the strength of her emotions. She didn't sound mad, exactly, more like she was trying to tell him the same thing repeatedly and he just wouldn't listen. She wasn't imperious, like Lila, but in her own way she was just as demanding.

Elizabeth doesn't lose track of why she's mad, Sam considered regretfully. It made her hard to distract.

"You know, Sam," she addressed him with an evident lack of patience, "it's not that you're such a screwup, which you're not. I don't blame you for wanting to stick to the syllabus and everything. It's just that you didn't have the decency, I mean the common decency, just to *tell* me about it. And instead I go along all week like a—" She paused.

Sam framed the doorknob with the camera and practiced zooming in and zooming out. He wished she'd just go ahead and open the door. "—no. I am not going to go into that with you,

Sam. I'm not going to go into the conversations I had with Ms. Barton or the time I put in on it. I am not even going to consider when you might possibly have first known that there was no way you were going to shoot a film at my school at any time. I'm done thinking about it, Sam, so if you don't mind, I'll stop talking about it too."

"Elizabeth," he said. "Please. I'm not kidding! I am *so* going to make a documentary on you and that school. Look, just open the door, I'll show you the camera. You don't use a tripod; you just run around like a lunatic with this electric sewing machine drilling into your head. It's cool. And the light and sound are built in, let me show you, so I wouldn't even need a crew. I just have to get the hang of these settings. It's like trying to play the drum and guitar and harmonica at the same time, whaddaya call it, a one-man band."

He groped in front of him with his one free hand for the built-in light source. It looked like a big flashbulb from the outside, but surprisingly it shot out a very bright, steady, and rather harsh bluish white light when illuminated. You weren't supposed to use it too much unless you had a backup battery, which he didn't.

On the other hand, he didn't have any film for

the camera, so what did he care if he had to recharge it all day before he returned it? *Might as well go all out*, he thought. His fingers slipped clumsily around the face of the camera as he struggled to locate the tiny, ridged plastic switches that controlled the sound and light modules. *Shed a little light on the subject here.* He was vaguely aware of feeling like a dork, but the thought didn't bother him.

Accidentally his fingers hit the switch that started the camera itself running: The shutter whirred, the reels turned rapidly, clicking like electric trains, and the (empty) film canisters began to rattle with the vibrations. Until then he had just been looking for the eyepiece. The light, which he was trying to turn on, didn't make any noise, but the enormous clatter of machinery going off next to his ear left Sam half deaf. He shouted over the noise to Elizabeth.

"Anyway, once I get this figured out, I can come down and shoot some stuff with the kids and everything. It'll be fun. I can just follow them around when they go run and pick their noses and stuff. Sorry. Paint and stuff. Whatever. The point is that there's no reason we can't get it going before too long. I have a feeling that the class assignments aren't exactly going to deplete all my time. This *is* good ol' OCC, after all, kicking in just the way I like it. I think I can get use of the editing suites for it too. Elizabeth? What say; come on?"

Elizabeth opened the door curiously. Seeing that Sam had framed her in the eyepiece, she put her hands on her hips and shot him a defiant glare. "Sam. This is not the time. Nice camera, actually, though," she said, stepping closer to take a look. Just then Sam found the light switch, and the bright electronic light shone suddenly full in her eyes. She squawked in protest and put her hands over her eyes. "Sam! You dip! Turn that thing off!" Her hair and skin glowed in a uniformly ghoulish hue.

"I can't," he said truthfully. He couldn't find the switch, and he was afraid to put down the camera. He had a few more minutes of operational time anyway. Finally there was enough light to see properly. Elizabeth stood in the hallway next to her bedroom door, which was closed almost all the way. She crossed her arms and spoke to Sam's exposed ear instead of looking into the lens. It made her seem blind to Sam as he observed her through the viewfinder lens. She was squinting uncomfortably against the light.

"Well," she intoned, "if you want to propose a plan to me for coming down to the school or anything else for this phase you're in, just do me a

223

favor and write it down and slip it under my door. I don't much feel like going out of my way for you right now, Sam, but if you're serious, you can write something up."

"Okay," Sam agreed. He was just happy she was speaking to him. "So, Ms. Wakefield, tell us, when did you first realize your housemate was a cinematic giant in the making?"

"Right after that flying pig came down the chimney," Elizabeth replied. "You remember, Sam. The one who had come in from hell after it froze over." She batted her eyes sarcastically at him.

"Wouldja look in the lens, Elizabeth?" he asked distractedly. She declined to cooperate and just stood there in the hall, irritated but bearing his presence.

She seemed to be permitting him to film her. Sam tried zooming in on her face and then panning back out to get a floor-to-ceiling shot. Elizabeth folded and refolded her arms over her chest and turned away. Her skin and hair were completely washed out by the overbright film light, leaving the shape of her jaw and nose to stand in the viewfinder like an abstract drawing.

Sam fiddled around a little on the lens for the f-stop adjustment. This was going to be impossible. But he lucked out and was able to find the tiny f-stop ring at the base of the lens. With this he was able to shrink the iris of the lens, which let in less light, which brought the image into recognizable form.

Regal, haughty, bored, long-suffering Elizabeth Wakefield appeared framed against the wall like a muted color-field painting, very few surfaces laid out in very few colors but instantly unmistakable in form. The light cords in her neck held out the scoop neckline of her T-shirt, which together with her neck and jaw looked like a vase made of highly polished marble. Her eyes were barely visible as glowing flecks in the dark area formed above the ghostly shining of her cheekbones. *They used to shoot actors in profile in the old days all the time,* Sam recalled reading in his textbook. *You had a good side and a bad side. Oh, get my good side,* he joked in his mind. Actors.

That's the difference, he thought. *She's not acting. She's just* being. *This is real life!*

For a moment in the hallway Sam actually imagined that he was making a documentary film about Elizabeth right there. No, not a *documentary,* just a *document. Elizabeth here now,* he said to himself in his mind as a little mantra. He tried to give his imagination full rein. From his hiding place behind the eye of the camera, he was able somehow to take her in, seeing what he would have thought was just her steady but patient irritation at him from somewhat of a third-person point of view.

He tried just to see her as a *person,* as if she were a complete, three-dimensional natural phenomenon, like a rock formation or a bank of clouds, and not just as a source of diversion or despair. As if her mute hostile glare wasn't really for him so much as it was for the world itself coming up short against her expectations constantly and cruelly. *Yeah,* he thought. *Cool.*

Elizabeth turned back to her room. "Well," she said. "I could offer a few more words about young Sam Burgess, but I wouldn't want my mother to see me talking like that on film. So I'll have to cut this interview short." She slipped into her room and shut the door behind her. Sam kept the lens pinned on the door, sure she would come back out. She didn't.

Undaunted, Sam turned off the camera, leaving on the light, and practiced framing and moving with the handheld camera around the dusky hallway until the battery began to give out, the light faded, and he was left in the near dark.

But he felt like a light had come on in him. He'd found what he wanted to do with his life. Unbelievable.

And no matter what problems he'd have with girls, no one could ever take that away from him. *Oh, man,* he thought. *What is life going to be like out of Slackerville?*

Probably pretty great.

Thought-book entry

Note: Get used to keeping better production notebooks.

Lila. At least she called me sexy, right? So I got that going for me now.

Whatever. From what I've seen so far, the film looks great, and that's all that really matters. As far as my love life goes, nothing's changed. Figures.

1. Chris—Never knew she existed until two weeks ago, so it's almost like we never met at all.

2. Lila—The thought itself was worth it.

3. Elizabeth—She's being civil to me again. Not making me any cheeseburgers, but at least she's not throwing things at me.

4. Lara Croft—The girl who's always there for me, waiting patiently for my visit on the ol' Boom Raider . . .

Check out the all-new....

Sweet Valley Web site—

www.sweetvalley.com

New Features

Cool Prizes

The ONLY official Web site!

Hot Links

And much more!

BFYR 202